Dead Mule Swamp
Singer

an Anastasia Raven mystery
Joan H. Young

DEDICATION

To:

Janice Lee Davis, who first introduced me to the mountain dulcimer on a trip to Alabama and even taught me how to play a song. With thanks for expanding my knowledge and enjoyment of life.

1

"We can pull this off. When someone wants to believe it's true, they trust you."

2

Chester Alan Arthur Schoellkopf was assuredly a hunk, if you liked aging hunks. Hunks who were a little too sure they represented a gift of the gods to the human race. But he was Adele's old friend. A "dear friend," she had confided, when she told me he was coming to visit, so I kept my opinions to myself.

Adele and I, and more than half the population of Cherry Hill, were at the Spring Strawberry Shortcake and Sundae Social– advertised as the 5S Sunday– being held on the lawn of the Lutheran church. It was a warm Memorial Day Sunday, May 29th that year, and despite stomachs being full of barbecued chicken and potato salad, the ice cream and strawberries were disappearing quickly. I was doing my part to prevent the unnecessary melting of any frozen dairy products. Chocolate syrup drizzled over the real whipped cream topping was the pinnacle of perfection.

Caught with a spoonful halfway to my mouth, Adele and Chester approached the folding chair where I was perched.

"Ana, meet Chester," Adele crooned. "I've been telling him all about you!"

I had to choose whether to delay the carefully balanced treat or go for it. Of course, I filled my pie hole. Or in this case, my ice-cream hole.

Chester smiled unctuously and held out a tanned but hairy paw. I replaced the spoon in my styrofoam bowl, set the remaining sundae on the grass beneath my chair and stood up so that we were meeting more as equals than as vassal to lord.

"Call me Chet," he said as we shook hands, and I quickly forced the cold ice cream down my throat.

"My pleasure," I choked out, hoping I wouldn't get brain freeze.

Chet was above average height, but not too tall. His tightly-curled blond hair was going gray, but the effect was of a silver-gold mixture that sparkled in the sunshine. Hair was his signature feature. Not only were his knuckles hairy, but he sported a full mustache in the middle of a long face. Two buttons of a creamy silk shirt were undone, and curly hairs rioted everywhere in the exposed triangle, leading me to believe the curl was natural. It would be a little too weird if he permed that. I wondered if the chunky gold chain he wore around his neck tangled enough to be painful. A square gold signet ring with a central diamond glittered on his right hand. His clothes were not synthetic, his shoes not imitation leather. Everything about Chet screamed money. Well, money and hair.

Adele beamed and offered some new information. "Chet has rented the apartment above the drugstore for at least a month. That's a nice place for our little downtown, with its own enclosed stairway. And it's furnished, too. I'm so happy to have him nearby. We have a lot of catching up to do."

She slipped her arm through Chet's, and he smiled down at Adele. They were an incongruous couple if that's what was happening here. Adele is at least matronly, if not downright heavy. She looks exactly like what she is, a middle-aged businesswoman who doesn't have time to worry about fashion or makeup. Her one nod to beauty is a trip to the hairdresser every couple of months for a wave and to catch up on the gossip she might have missed. Not that she misses much.

Out of the corner of my eye, I saw my young friend, Jimmie Mosher, walking toward us. He wore a black apron embroidered with a cluster of pink flowers and the words Cherry Blossom Cuisine. Clipped to the strap of his apron was a set of car keys. Jimmie was justifiably proud of his new driver's license, even though it would be provisional for a few more months.

"Hi Ana," he called. Then, realizing he might be interrupting, he stopped and waited for further encouragement.

I waved him in. "Come meet Mr. Schoellkopf, Jimmie."

Then, to Chet I said, "This is my buddy. Adele's too."

Adele had long been a friend to Jimmie, so they were on a first name basis. In the year when Jimmie was picking up and selling scrap metal from roadsides to feed himself, he would often leave her store, Volger's Grocery, with a bit more food than his pocket change technically covered. But Adele was wise enough to refrain from giving him items for free. She would claim the label on a can was ripped, or the produce was old. I'd actually seen her smush a loaf of bread on the sly so she could sell it to Jimmie as damaged. Adele may be a busy-body, but her heart is pure gold.

Jimmie and Chester shook hands.

"So, young man, you work for the caterer who made these shortcakes? Excellent baking, and the strawberries are the rosy perfection of sunshine."

"Thank you, Mr. Schoellkopf," Jimmie said as a sly smile spread across his face. "Actually, the business is mine, although it has to be registered in my mom's name until I'm eighteen. We all pitch in. Sometimes my little sisters help too, but dishing up ice cream is simple. They get today off."

"Wonderful. Amazing," Chet gushed. "What drew you to the food services, young man?"

"My dad used to own the Cherry Blossom Restaurant out on the highway. Do you know it?"

Chet shook his head in the negative.

"Well, it's a wreck now. Dad was killed in a car accident when I was a baby, and the building was lost in a tax sale. But Mom and I are hoping we can buy it back. I want to re-open it. The Pine Tree Diner is great for a sandwich, but there's no place in the whole county to dine out in style any more."

"I'll have to check it out. The Pine Tree is all right, but not quite what I'm used to. I'll be in town for a month. I don't suppose you'll be up and running by then."

Jimmie grinned at the obvious teasing. "No sir. It's not likely."

Everyone chuckled. My ice cream was melting.

Jimmie turned to me. "Ana, do you think maybe you can help us take some of the equipment back to our house when this is over? The portable freezers take up a lot of space. We can't get it all in one trip, even with the van, and Lindsey has a piano lesson at four."

"Sure, Jimmie," I replied.

"Great, thanks!" He headed back toward the serving tables.

I glanced sideways at my sundae, sat down and rescued it. Definitely softer now, but still edible.

"Chet and I hope you'll join us for some outings," Adele said.

"I'd like that," I said, digging my spoon into the deflating mound of dessert and hoping they would get the message that this conversation was over.

"Looking forward to it," Chet agreed, running slim fingers across his mustache, then patting Adele's arm, still linked in his.

As Adele steered Chet in the direction of someone else she wanted to introduce, I had to wonder what was going on. Adele usually stuck tight to her store, watched television in the evenings, kept tabs on everyone, and ran the Family Friends Committee at Cornerstone Fellowship where we attended church. Her husband, Henry, had died long before I moved to Cherry Hill, and I'd never seen her show any interest in another man. I like Adele, and Chester seemed oily. I felt a tinge of concern.

3

The annual Strawberry Social was a big deal in Cherry Hill, and I wouldn't have missed it for anything, but it was people-intense for my tastes. Funny how I'd changed. I used to live in a suburb of Chicago. I had a busy life teaching literature at a community college and thought my marriage to an upper level manager of a chain store was solid, if not exactly great. I was always involved in social gatherings. But Roger had informed me he was in love with someone named Brian. In shock, I'd bought the last house on a dead-end road several miles outside of a very small town, miles and miles north of the Windy City. I wasn't sure it would work out, but I had to make some big changes to be able to move forward. In retrospect, the decision was just perfect. Now, I valued the privacy and enjoyed a few close friendships. Roger got his freedom, and I got enough money to create my new life.

That evening, I was relaxing in my upstairs screened porch that overlooks Dead Mule Swamp. I'd taken the winter shutters off only the week before. Spring in the Northwoods is fickle before Memorial Day. I was more than ready for warm evenings simmered in slanting light and the cheerful chorusing of peepers and vesper sparrows.

The sky to the west was turning pink, and the light spread across the swamp, causing every puddle of open water to glow with the pink satin of early roses. The trees were barely leafing out, so the reflections shimmered and winked as small gusts of the light breeze stirred the nascent greenery. Beyond the swamp ran the Petite Sauble River. But that was too far for me to ever see from the house. I could trace its course on chilly mornings by the line of mist that rose beyond the trees.

I'd discovered the foundations of an old cabin near the shore of the river on my property. Last summer, my son, Chad, who was now looking for his first post-college job, had rebuilt the small structure. Just one room, but it was a wonderful place to camp when the mosquitoes weren't too obnoxious. We'd added a fire ring and benches. My kayak was stored inside, and I hoped to build some bunks this summer. Although this section of the river was not generally popular with paddlers, I could work my way through the braided backwaters whenever I wanted to. I'd enjoyed some birdwatching forays in the little-visited area.

The breeze was dying down, and the peaceful quiet seeped into my bones. This, this was why a fixer-upper house on the back side of nowhere was right for me.

"Deep river, ... home ...over Jordan." Snatches of an old spiritual drifted from the direction of the river. The voice was male and deep, but not bass. More like a rich baritone.

Must be someone trying to paddle down from the Turtle Lake Dam to Cherry Hill, I thought. Spring, when the water was high, was about the only time of year anyone had a very good chance of making it through. Most of the time, there were shallow spots netted with sandbars. Snags and deadfalls meant that anyone trying to paddle this section had to watch carefully and do a lot of extemporaneous portaging. In some places it was almost impossible to tell where the main channel was, and as a result, people sometimes got lost back in the swamp. But not usually ones who calmly sang spirituals. And not usually at sunset. The swamp could be dangerous after dark. Soft sand, unexpectedly deep pools, broken winter trees hung up and waiting to fall if disturbed all threatened anyone who went astray.

I hoped the man was just passing by and knew what he was doing.

"Oh, don't you want to go-o to that Gospel feast..." The voice was now coming from upstream of its previous location. That was definitely odd. Hardly anyone paddled upstream. Even more remarkable was that the voice was now accompanied by some stringed instrument. A guitar? It didn't sound quite right. An autoharp? I barely knew what that was, but I didn't think it was capable of the complex notes I was hearing that blew to me in snatches of sound.

"To that promised land where all is peace. Deep river..." These words were followed by an instrumental interlude. Then it came to me. No one can paddle and play something that requires two hands at the same time. A radio? More than one person? The paddler had stopped somewhere?

In fact, the music was definitely coming from the general direction of my cabin. Should I have concerns about some mystery singer? Who could it be?

Chester Alan Arthur Schoellkopf– Adele had made sure I knew his whole name– was the only stranger in town that I knew of. Was he a closet crooner? More likely, I was hearing holiday weekend vacationers oblivious to the dangers of the river after dark.

This is ridiculous, I said to myself, swinging my legs off the ottoman on which they had been resting. It took me a couple of minutes to find and put on my sneakers. Then I grabbed a light jacket and ran down the stairs. It was dark enough by this time to want a flashlight, but finally I was working my way down the compacted pathway that led to the cabin.

"Who's there?" I called as I entered the clearing, swinging the light in arcs across the opening and throwing shadows everywhere.

No one was there. I saw no drag marks on the bank where a canoe or kayak might have pulled up. There were no obvious footprints. I checked the lock on the cabin door, shrugged and headed back to the house.

4

Even towns as small as Cherry Hill have parades on Memorial Day. Ours began at the former school, now the museum, owned and operated by my friend Cora Caulfield. I arrived at nine in the morning and parked in the lot across the street which was already nearly full of cars and trucks. Cherry Hill seemed like such a sleepy town, but for events like this people came from all around.

The veterans were checking their uniforms and shining the toes of their boots by rubbing them against the backs of their pant legs. Boy Scouts directed cars to park in orderly rows. The Girl Scouts had a float with the international trefoil glittering in plastic gold fringe against a blue wrapping-paper background. Daisy and Brownie Scouts sat on the edges of the wagon. In the center were girls dressed in historic uniforms. I smiled as I recognized one I had worn as a child.

The clown was already handing out candy. Horses pranced nervously. The Cornerstone Fellowship float was pulling into position behind the Girl Scouts. Local Chief of Police, Tracy Jarvi, held a sheet of paper she kept referencing. She motioned people closer, looked at her notes and pointed them to the correct locations following a numbered code chalked on the road.

Cora exited the front door of the museum, saw me, and hustled to my side. For the patriotic occasion, she wore a red-and-blue shirt covered with white stars beneath her faded denim overalls. I'd seen Cora in something other than overalls twice. Maybe three times. I almost forgot about Cliff Sorenson's funeral. That seemed so far in the past, and yet it had been only five years since I'd come here, and Cliff had died. Now, so many of these people were known to me, meant something to me. It made my feelings about Chester Schoellkopf, the outsider, pulsate. He looked like a first-class con man, and I didn't want him to be here for the purpose of cheating any of my friends.

"We sure hated to miss the ice cream social yesterday," Cora said, "but we had to go visit Jerry's grandson. He and his wife just had a baby. A girl. We got home last night."

I knew that Jerry Caulfield's family was something of a sore spot. The Caulfields had founded the county newspaper in 1876, but none of Jerry's children or grandchildren wanted to carry on the tradition. Jerry, as owner and editor, was perhaps facing the end of *The Cherry Hill Herald* when he did decide it was time to give it up. Finding a buyer without selling out to a big syndicate was going to be problematic. And he'd never sell to a syndicate. I imagined seeing the baby was a treat, but also that there might have been painful conversations with the parents.

The floats were all in place, the middle school band led out, playing the "Cherry Blossom Rag," and slowly each participant group began to roll or walk east on Liberty Street toward Mill Street, the main drag. Cora and I walked too, keeping pace with the parade.

"Doesn't the museum have a float?" I asked.

"Not this year. I just couldn't do it, not knowing exactly when that baby would arrive. It's OK. They are a lot of work. Floats. Well, babies too, but this one isn't mine, thank goodness."

We all turned south on Mill Street. This was where most of the spectators lined the curbs. American flags fluttered. Children screamed as candy flew in their direction. The mayor waved from the convertible driven by Cora's husband, Jerry Caulfield. He must have been recruited to drive as soon as they returned to town.

As we passed City Park, we saw Adele and her newcomer friend standing in the grassy opening, crowded among all the other spectators.

Cora doesn't miss a beat. "Who's that?" she asked.

Of course, she was referring to Chet. Everyone else was known to us.

"That," I said, "is Chester Alan Arthur Schoellkopf. He's Adele's old friend. I met him yesterday."

"Humph, he looks like more than a friend," Cora observed as Chet bent over and whispered in Adele's ear. Even from the other side of the street, we could see Adele blush.

We waited until the tail end of the parade passed– the high school band playing "Stars and Stripes Forever." Then we crossed to join Adele and Chet.

Introductions were made, and I told them about hearing someone singing in Dead Mule Swamp the previous evening. Chet never flinched. If he was the mystery paddler, he covered his guilt like a pro.

"Memorial Day vacationers," Adele declared. "They'll go anywhere, whether it makes any sense or not."

"Make sure your cabin is secure. The shed behind Aho's Service Station was broken into on Thursday," Cora added.

Spectators were moving toward their cars, or else walking along behind the parade. The goal was the cemetery on the south end of town where a short service honoring the military dead would be held. Adele and Chet climbed into his vehicle, a silver Special Edition Jeep. Adele could barely step that high, but Chet assisted her. They offered us a ride, but Cora and I decided to walk.

"What on earth has gotten into her?" Cora demanded, as soon as the Jeep had pulled away.

"Beats me. I haven't heard the whole story, but I guess they used to date long ago. He called her last week, and here he is."

Cora sniffed. "You mark my words. There's something shady about him. Too much gold for Cherry Hill. I'll bet it's all for show, and he's after Adele's money. She has some, you know."

I hadn't known that. We continued toward the cemetery in quiet companionship.

***

The evening wasn't nearly as balmy as on the previous night. A raw fog settled down over the swamp, and I turned the lights on early. I was wrapped in a blanket and reading a book when I heard the metallic strumming music again. This time, I wasn't going to wait. It was definitely coming from the direction of the cabin, and I was quicker getting out the door.

Once again, I ran down the path, flashlight in hand. Once again, I called out as I approached the clearing. And, once again, no one was there. I checked the cabin lock, which was fine. Nothing seemed to have been disturbed. The fog dampened and dispersed all sounds, making me doubt that the song had really come from the area of the cabin.

A Memorial Day vacationer? That didn't seem likely. He would have headed home by Monday evening of the long weekend.

Whoever it was probably saw my flashlight bobbing through the trees and had plenty of time to fade back into the woods, or paddle on. In any event, the fog would have hidden him this evening. I thought about installing a security cam, but I'd never needed one before. Technology and I aren't friends. It would take more than a disembodied voice to motivate me to make a purchase like that.

I waited a few minutes then walked back to my house, wondering if I should be concerned or not.

5

Tuesday, it was back to business as usual. My Tuesday routine included working with Cora at the museum to continue adding entries to the huge database of inventoried items that she was building.

We didn't have a chance to visit as much as we often do. Cora was preoccupied with working on a schedule for the high school work-study students who wanted to continue to volunteer at the museum throughout the summer. She explained that school was dismissing for the summer very soon, and she was making that job a priority.

My project of the day was to start entering the salt and pepper shaker collection donated by Mrs. Mildred "Bunny" Hungerford. I raised my eyebrows when Cora said "salt and pepper shakers," but this was a stunning collection from around the world. Granted, there were the expected smiling cows and kissing Dutch children, but I also unpacked majolica owls, antique pewter pairs, and Fostoria crystal sets. Bunny had done us a great service because each set was catalogued with information about where and when she had acquired it.

Even Cora's lifetime collection of anything old and interesting from Forest County hadn't yet filled the entire pre-consolidation school building that now housed the museum, so I was sure the cows and the crystal would somehow be displayed.

Noon came, and I was hungry. Cora was still tied up, so I headed to the Pine Tree Diner. Jack Panther makes the best tuna melt I've ever eaten. The diner is only six small-town blocks from the museum, so I walked.

Much to my surprise, Adele was seated at one of the booths. I had expected she would be on the floor at Volger's Grocery. Her usual lunch is a quick sandwich eaten in the office at the store. Once I processed that Adele was there, it was no surprise at all that she was seated beside Chester. There was a third person across the table from them, a man who seemed to be a genetic duplicate of Chester, only much younger. And wearing less gold. He was deeply tanned, proving he either had recently arrived in the north or that he frequented tanning parlors. His hair was blond and curly too. He had a beard, but all his hair was neatly trimmed. He was wearing a bold blue-and-yellow Hawaiian print shirt. Except for the beard, he looked exactly like an actor from a 1970s surfer movie. Adele waved me over to join them, although it was clear they were well into lunch already.

As I slid into the seat, Chester– I decided right then that I couldn't bring myself to think of him with the familiarity of "Chet"– began loudly introducing the other man.

"Ana, this is Tucker Schoellkopf, my grandson. It seems he's been chasing me all over the country and finally caught up with me in your jerkwater burg."

Adele cringed just the tiniest bit at the derisive label slapped on the village she loved, but she didn't say a word.

"Pleased to meet you," Tucker said, twisting on the bench and reaching to shake my hand.

"Ana writes for the *Cherry Hill Herald*," Adele said. "The crime beat usually, but Tucker has a fascinating story. I'm sure the paper would be interested."

"Yes, my head is reeling," Chester said. "Although I'm highly pleased at what I've been hearing."

"Fill me in," I said, leaning forward. Although, since there were other diners in the Pine Tree, I was sure the whole town would know about Tucker before the weekly paper came out the next day, Wednesday. Unless this was some sort of fantastic tale that I'd need to write up quickly and get to Jerry in the next couple of hours, and for which he'd have to rearrange the layout and delay the press, the printed news would be a week late.

Jack Panther approached with a glass of water and a cup of strong black coffee–he knows me well–and took my order. The Pine Tree does require more than one person to operate, but Jack likes to wait on some of us personally.

While I sipped coffee and anticipated warm tuna and cheese on rye, Chester talked.

"It turns out that my son, Lyle, had another child none of us previously knew about," he began.

"Another child?" I asked.

"Well, there's Eva," Chester replied, "But she doesn't count."

The others had apparently heard this already. They didn't react. It was up to me to ask for more information.

"How's that?"

Adele answered *sotto voce,* although I was sure everyone in the diner had already heard. "Chester disinherited her several years ago. She hasn't been seen since."

I raised my eyebrows. "So where have you been, Tucker?"

"Me?" the young man asked. "Hawaii. Grew up there. It's where my mother lived. I've never been this far north. I'm freezing." He shivered.

If the boy, for he was certainly barely out of his teens, was so cold, I wondered why he didn't put on a sweater and long pants. Maybe he didn't bring any with him.

"There's a thrift shop run by the Catholic Church," I said, "and larger stores in Emily City. Maybe you should buy a jacket."

My meal arrived. I thanked the girl who delivered it and took a big bite of the delicious sandwich.

"We'll run over to the city this afternoon and do some shopping," Chester said. "Tucker used all his ready cash to track me down."

Already the boy was mooching. I swallowed. "What proof does Tucker have that he's related to you?"

"Just look at him," Chester boomed.

I had to admit the resemblance was uncanny.

"He has some paperwork as well," Adele added.

Tucker pulled two items from a file folder he had stashed between his hip and the wall. One was a piece of paper, the other was a photograph.

"This is Lyle, my father, and me as a baby," Tucker said, pushing the faded square image toward me.

I looked at Chester, and he nodded. "That's Lyle all right."

"Show her the test results," Adele urged.

Tucker shook open the document. "I bought one of those DNA kits. See here," he pointed at a line of print, "'Father, Lyle Schoellkopf; grandfather, Chester Alan Arthur Schoellkopf.' I never really knew Lyle. His affair with my mother didn't last long, but now that I've had the test done, there's no doubt."

6

"Let me see that snapshot again," I requested.

I flipped it over, but there was nothing on the back. The faded print had a bent corner and was clearly of an age. The toys in the picture were ones my own son had played with around 1990. I recognized a Beanie Baby and something with Big Bird on it. I'd learned from many hours spent with Cora in the museum that even if a photo had no date, sometimes you could determine a narrow window for when the picture had been taken just by clues both from the items in the photo and by how well the photographic chemicals had held up.

A man sat on the steps in front of a vinyl-sided house. A bald toddler stood in the grass facing him. You could not see the child's face. The stocky man in the snapshot did not look much like Chester or Tucker. His hair was straight and dark.

"You're sure this is your son?" I asked Chester while placing a finger on the man in the photo.

"Oh, absolutely, Chester replied. "He took after his mother."

To Tucker, I said, "Where was this picture taken?"

"No clue," the young man replied, lifting an eyebrow. "I'm hardly old enough to remember the day."

I looked at Chester.

He shook his head. "I don't recognize that house either. That lends some weight to Tucker's claim, I think. If Lyle had an affair, he certainly wouldn't have brought the baby anywhere near his wife, or the rest of us, for that matter."

I smelled fish, and it wasn't my tuna sandwich, which I wanted to finish eating.

"Tell me about yourself, Chester. Start with your name. It seems a little outrageous."

Chester Alan Arthur Schoellkopf leaned back into the corner of the booth, lifted his chin and laughed. "Oh, it is. It is! But catchy, don't you think?"

Adele was smiling and nodding her head. Clearly, she'd heard this tale before.

Chester began, "My father was a big fan of the twenty-first President of the United States. Arthur was never elected, you know."

"What nonsense is that?" Tucker asked.

"No nonsense at all. Several Presidents were never elected. You should have at least heard of Gerald R. Ford. He was never even elected to the Vice-presidency."

"Yeah, I know that name," Tucker said, "but I'm not a big history buff."

When a President dies and the VP ascends, he becomes the Chief Executive. But at the end of the term, he might choose not to run again, or his opponent might win. In either case, you have a president who was never elected. The first such President was John Tyler who took power when that ego-maniac William Henry Harrison gave a four-hour acceptance speech in the rain, caught pneumonia and died. In the 1840s that was."

"So, you're into politics?" Tucker asked.

"Not really, it was my father who followed it all. But with this name, I've had to learn a few facts to hold my own against those who snicker."

"That makes sense," I commented.

"He was teased a lot in college," Adele added. "Chester was not a popular name in the 1970s."

Chester patted Adele's arm and continued, "Anyway, the other good old Chester became the Prez when Garfield was assassinated by a lawyer who thought Garfield owed him a political favor. Chester A. Arthur got off to a rocky start, but actually turned out to be a pretty good leader for the country. Lots of integrity– a tough stance to pull off in high positions. Even Mark Twain praised his accomplishments."

Tucker snorted. "If he was so great, how come he didn't get re-elected."

"He didn't run. Poor health. Some kidney disease. He was dead a year later."

Tucker shook his head, "Kind of strange, naming a baby for a dead guy."

"Not at all. Babies are named for famous people all the time. Hey, at least I wasn't named for a horse thief."

There was a moment of silence as everyone seemed to be processing the presidential stories or perhaps trying to think of a famous horse thief.

Chester recovered first. He seemed to be quite a talker. "Even your... what? Your half sister was named for an actress. Her mother just loved Eva Gabor in that TV show. I forget the name."

"Green Acres," Adele supplied.

"Tell me about Eva," Tucker said.

Now Chester looked less pleased. "Shouldn't have brought her up," he said under his breath.

Tucker shifted positions and smiled. "Well, she is my half sister. I'd like to meet her."

Chester slapped the table, and other diners lifted their heads and looked our way in surprise. "No one here is meeting that good-for-nothing brat if I can help it," he barked.

Adele grabbed Chester's hand. "You're making a scene! Calm down."

Chester wrenched away and looked at Adele. "I'm serious. She had seventeen years to prove she could be a worthy Schoellkopf, but what did she do? Threw it all away. Got into illegal substances. Ran off with a motorcycle gang. She could be strung out in a Mexican jail for all I know. Haven't seen her in years, and I'm fine with it. Lyle disappeared after that. Nobody has heard from him either. My wife died years ago. You'd better believe all my money is going to charities."

His eyes became bright. He took a deep breath and turned toward Tucker. "Well, maybe now that I have a grandson..."

Tucker smiled, his teeth gleaming through his beard. "What shall I call you?"

"Call me Chet, son. We are going to be great pals, you and me."

7

I stopped at the grocery store before heading south out of town. Adele still hadn't returned, but the register was being adequately manned by a college student. There was always a good supply of young people who attended Sturgeon Community College in Emily City who were also looking for work.

Loaded down with fresh fruits and veggies for a big salad and some hamburger, I was hopeful that for once I'd bought enough food to last me several days. Meal preparedness is not my strong suit. Just ask Adele or Cora.

As I drove home, I thought about the discussion at the diner. In reality, I'd learned very little about Chester. The history lesson was educational, but not very personal. Still, Adele knew him. He certainly wasn't some impostor posing as a long-lost friend. Tucker, on the other hand, was a complete mystery. There was something just a little too peculiar about both Chester and Tucker showing up in Cherry Hill within days of each other. Maybe I was being overly suspicious because Chester wanted Tucker to be his grandson very badly. And who could blame him? If his only known grandchild had gone off the rails, no wonder he was hopeful of someone to carry on his bloodline.

The afternoon was beautiful– warm and sunny with just a tiny bit of chill remaining in the air. I suspected there were still some small patches of ice in the swamp, even though it was nearly June. I got out the rake and started working on the flower beds. An adult ed course I'd taken at the community college had taught that raking too early destroyed cocoons of beneficial butterflies. The leaf litter also returned nutrients to the soil.

My rural kingdom in Forest County had not yet reached the stage where I was actually designing and planting flower beds, but a few perennials struggled to survive near the foundation of the house, and I tried to keep them happy. Besides, the exercise felt good.

By 5:30 the yard was clear. I grabbed a beer from the fridge and headed to my second-story screened porch. Collapsing in the white wicker chair and putting my feet up on the matching ottoman, I sighed. Life had been good to me in the past few years. I loved this house. I'd fixed up every room with the exception of the kitchen. Its peeling yellowed wallpaper with twining ivy was probably sixty years old, and the early Formica counter tops were chipped and stained. I really needed to start planning that renovation project. But it would be huge. It would make almost as much mess as when I had added this upstairs porch and my project room. Currently popular stainless steel appliances didn't really fit the character of the rest of the house. But what did? Kitchens and food interested me so much less than other things. That indifference had spilled over into ignoring the room that needed a makeover the most.

My mind wandered to thoughts of my young friend, Jimmie Mosher. His great-great-grandfather had built the house I now lived in, and the barn, too. But the barn and sheds had long ago faded into the weeds. Part of the reason I'd met Jimmie was because of his family ties to this property.

The can of beer was slipping from my fingers. I guided it to the floor so it wouldn't spill on the bright tropical print cushions. My shoulders relaxed.

***

Someone was playing a guitar. Chords combined in pleasing harmonies, and a deep voice pulsed in swells and troughs like waves rocking a boat. I jerked awake. It was not a guitar, but that strange resonating metallic instrument I'd heard before. I recognized the tune of "I'll Fly Away." There was no remaining light outside, and I couldn't see the stars. Clouds must have rolled in.

I stood and moved close to the screen, grabbing an afghan to wrap around my shoulders. The night had cooled off considerably, and a light breeze was carrying sounds to me.

Well, after all, why should I care if someone was singing out by the river? It didn't even matter if they had beached at my cabin and were sitting on my rough benches, did it? At least they were on key. In fact, as words were added to the tune, I heard, "when the shadows of this life have flown, I'll fly away. Like a bird from prison bars has flown... Just a few more weary days and then..."

The Dead Mule Swamp singer had a beautiful voice but he seemed to be enveloped in a deep sadness as well as shrouded in mystery. I remained at the screen, listening quietly. There were no lights glittering through the trees. Whoever was out there was playing in the velvet darkness. The song ended; a few random chords were strummed, and then a loud crashing crack broke the silence.

A yell... dry rustling as someone was running through last year's fallen leaves–then there was silence again.

Should I call someone? It would take a Sheriff's car twenty minutes to arrive. Although the Cherry Hill Police Chief, Tracy Jarvi, was my good friend, I lived outside her jurisdiction. She couldn't justify running out here, and, anyway, that would take almost as long as the county unit. I had no close neighbors.

Whoever was there had run away, right? But what if someone else had assaulted the singer? My melancholy musician didn't seem dangerous. He could be lying there, hurt.

I grabbed my jacket and a first aid kit. I even remembered to put the cell phone in my pocket. I hunted around for the large flashlight and eventually recalled that I had left it in the Jeep. It was probably almost ten minutes before I was, for the third time, walking the path to the cabin after dark.

"Is anyone there?" I called, yet again. No answer.

Entering the clearing, I directed the light in large arcs, quickly taking in the scene. I saw no one. Now I played the light more carefully, searching the ground for someone who might be lying still, unconscious. I circled the cabin, throwing the beam of light first to the forest floor and then into the trees, watching for shadows that might waver out of sync with the movement of the flashlight. My ears were fine-tuned to catch any unusual sounds.

No cigarette smoke or heavy cologne lingered to mingle with the odors of damp earth and early greenery.

At the water line there was almost a beach. Most of the river's edge had a bank that was anywhere from a foot to three feet high, depending on the water level. However, either by nature or tool, here the land sloped to the water, making it possible to land a small boat. And tonight there were definite signs that someone had been here. A long keel scrape was visible; a canoe or kayak had been pulled up out of the water and had rested there long enough for water to drip from the gunwales and create two lines of small round pockmarks in the sandy soil. Footprints, larger than my own, indicated a person had recently pushed off into the river.

I played the light up and down the Petite Sauble. Reflections bounced back at me from riffles in the water. Two yellow eyes were momentarily captured, and then a raccoon humped its way across a log and disappeared into the trees with more rustling of leaves. Could that have been what I heard? No, I had definitely heard human footfalls.

Returning to the cabin, I once again checked to see if it was secure. The latch was broken, the jamb was splintered, and the door hung at a slight angle. The spade that was usually propped against the wall lay on the ground in front of the plastic doormat.

With my toe, I pushed the door open. The cabin wasn't really furnished yet. I'd stored the picnic table inside for the winter along with my kayak and a few general supplies. The table was in there. The kayak was not.

Angrily, I pulled out my cell and punched in 9-1-1.

8

Harvey Brown, a friend as well as a deputy, was on duty, and we chatted as we walked from my house back to the cabin. A young technician he'd brought along took pictures of the damage and made casts of a couple of the footprints. I texted a picture of the kayak to Harvey's phone.

"There's not a lot else we can do right now, Ana," he said. "But we'll keep our ears open."

"What about fingerprints," I asked.

This rough-sawn wood won't hold any. Ditto for the picnic table. Maybe if the top was polyurethaned, but this is just raw lumber."

He was right. I hadn't gotten around to finishing it yet.

"I'll bag the spade and take it back to the lab," the younger man said. "We might get lucky there.

***

I went to bed feeling violated and confused. The last time there was trouble with someone lurking in the swamp behind my house, that person was connected to a cold case that really had nothing to do with me personally. That's when the clearing had been discovered along with the foundation of some previous cabin. Had the former owner dismantled the building because of problems such as this? Maybe there was more river "traffic" than I realized.

As I lay in bed, it came to me that there must have been more than one person involved in the disappearance of my kayak. If the singer came by water, which I was reasonably sure was true, then he couldn't have paddled two boats when he left. Well, he might have tied them together and towed one, but there was definitely only one drag mark in the bare earth of the bank. Someone might have had another vessel stashed in the woods, and launched from a less visible location.

***

As I drank my required three cups of morning coffee, I decided on an immediate course of action. I could find out more about canoe rentals and access points. And I wanted to do so in person. I like to see the face of the person I'm questioning.

This meant that the day would start with a pleasant late springtime drive over to Kirtland Road within Thousand Lakes State Forest, to the far northeast side of Turtle Lake. Since it was post-Memorial Day, I assumed the rental would be open, and as I pulled into the gravel parking area, I saw that I was correct.

A young man, probably also a college student on summer break, smiled through an access window as I approached the shack that served as an office. The plastic name tag pinned to his polo shirt read "Buck." The window was just an opening in one side of the building. A top-hinged shutter was propped up to provide an awning for customers.

"Looking for a kayak this morning?" Buck asked. His eyes wandered to take in my jeans and sneakers. "You might prefer paddling in shorts."

I smiled back. No sense in antagonizing him right away. "No playtime for me today. Sorry. I'd like to ask you a couple of questions, though."

"Sure. Fire away. But I just started work yesterday."

Mentally rolling my eyes, I began. "Do you do rentals for people who want to canoe on the river. Say, below the dam?"

"We do," he said. "We'll transport your car to where you want to take out, and then put you in up-river. That said, there aren't very many good stretches in there. What do you have in mind?"

"Actually, I'm interested in knowing if there have been any recent rentals for that purpose, say in the last week."

"Can't tell you. I'm not even sure I'd be allowed to tell you. Hang on. I'll find Zed."

A side door opened in the shed, and the college boy stepped out into the sunshine. He was pasty-pale, as we all were at this time of year. Well, all except Chet and Tucker. Why were they both so tanned? Had they come from the same part of the country? Tucker had mentioned Hawaii.

This young man's cargo shorts were sagging on his skinny hips and he wore a backwards Detroit Tigers baseball cap. He pointed in the direction of a rack of colorful canoes and kayaks, behind which was a larger building.

As we walked in that direction, he yelled, "Zed! Lady here's got a question."

An older man appeared, covered in cobwebs. He wiped dirty hands on the front of his denim coveralls and extended one in my direction. Then he looked at the still-dirty hand and thought better of it.

"What c'n I do for ya?" he asked.

I recognized him as the person who had rented me a kayak a few times, before I'd bought one of my own. I repeated my questions to him.

"Not really supposed to tell people that kinda stuff. But can't see there's any harm in tellin' you that nobody's ordered a river trip from us yet this year. We'd discourage it anyway. Water's high and fast. Nobody's cut out the snags yet."

"Does the river get cleared most years?" I asked.

"Not officially on most of it. People do it on their own authority. DNR gits tired of rescuin' folks who get lost in those backwaters. But there is a stretch just below the dam that's pretty popular. 'Bout a three-hour float dependin' on the current. We encourage people to take out at the mouth of the Thorpe. Below that... well, it's a mess. Above there, yeah, it gets cleaned up for safety reasons."

I thanked Zed and the young man for the information. I knew the takeout at the Thorpe. It was at the end of the seasonal road that extended past my house. But the vehicle access was from the east side of the river, so I never saw cars driving there.

"Say, I think I know who you are," Zed said, pointing a dirty finger at me and grinning. "You're that lady who writes for the paper. Got mixed up in most every crime in the county these last few years, ain'tcha?"

It was true, and I acknowledged both facts.

Buck's eyes widened, and Zed snorted. "You lookin' fer another body along the river?"

"No, definitely not," I stated.

9

"Come back any time you're ready for a little paddling," Buck invited.

I answered too quickly. "Thanks, but I have my own kayak now." Then I remembered. "Well, I did have. It was stolen last night."

"Dang kids never have enough to keep 'em busy," Zed said, pounding his fist against the side of the maintenance building.

Buck asked, "What kind and color?"

"It's an Old Town Otter. Red."

Zed snorted again, "Only a couple-uh thousand of those in the state, but we can keep an eye peeled."

I thanked them and drove in to town.

My first stop was at Jouppi's Hardware where I bought a new hasp and lock for my cabin. Then I headed to the lumber yard to buy a few boards. But mostly, I wanted to see Adele, and today, she was where I expected to find her–in the office at Volger's Grocery.

Adele had refinished the wooden front door that squealed on its hinges when you opened it. She was committed to preserving the small-town atmosphere of Cherry Hill. I approved and used this door most of the time just because I liked it. On the side of the building, off a vacant lot turned parking area was a modern sliding glass double door for accessibility. But from the front, you might still imagine it was 1900. The big maple tree that was buckling the sidewalk was nearly leafed out, and it cast a green glow beneath its branches. I pushed open the door which jiggled a small bell to signal my entrance.

Leaning sideways to peer through the large plate glass window of her office, Adele motioned me to join her. I slipped into the fishbowl and closed the door behind me.

"Ana. I have so much to tell you," she began.

"I have news too," I countered. "You first."

"Chet is taking me to Cold Rapids this weekend for a concert. Isn't that divine? I made a special appointment to have my hair done on Friday."

This was definitely not the Adele I knew. Most evenings she contentedly watched the news and a series of favorite television shows.

"We're going on Saturday. We'll have a nice meal somewhere. He wants to surprise me, and then he's got tickets to the symphony."

"Wow! Who's watching the store?"

"You remember Suzi Preston, right? She's home for the summer, and she knows the business well enough to do the dailies. I've hired her. Maybe it's time I stopped spending all day, every day, here. She can supervise Max, too." She nodded in the direction of the young man at the cash register who was waiting on a shopper.

My warning sensors were still beeping like crazy when it came to Chester, but it wouldn't do to tell Adele this just yet. I didn't want her to stop confiding in me. "That sounds very nice. I agree that you don't have enough chances to get out of town."

"You'll help me pick out something to wear, won't you?

Wondering if Adele had suddenly forgotten that my fashion sense was pretty marginal, I nodded agreement.

What's up with you?" she asked.

I explained about my evening visits from a baritone singer who played a mysterious instrument with strings and about the theft of my kayak.

"That just doesn't make much sense," Adele said.

"Why not? It happened just like that. And the kayak had to have disappeared yesterday. The lock on the cabin was fine when I checked it on Monday."

Adele shook her head. "Oh, I'm not questioning what you've told me. But so few people venture into that section of the river.

The name 'Dead Mule Swamp' didn't stick because it was a welcoming place."

"I've heard it's not popular," I agreed. "But maybe there are stretches that are familiar to someone. After all, I explored some of those backwaters last summer and they can be very pretty."

"Of course, Ana, but that's because you've learned how to find your way through. The river is so braided that everyone local has a story to tell about getting lost back there."

I laughed. "If 'everyone' has a story, then I guess it's been busy from time to time."

"Oh, mostly kids, you know. Lovers looking for privacy."

"There were the drug deals and Larry Louma, too, but that was a long time ago."

Adele nodded. "It was, but I suspect there are still some illegal shenanigans left for the new generation."

I was contemplating those possibilities when Adele leaned over and rapped on the office window. Max looked at her, startled, and pointed a finger at his chest.

Adele opened the office door and poked her head out. "If there are no customers in the store, you need to be checking the deli case to be sure there are to-go containers of every salad, and that the sandwiches are fresh. Check the aisles for trash or spills. Make yourself useful, young man." She extended her hand, palm down, and made motions to shoo her employee away.

I was pretty sure Max wasn't going to have time for any shenanigans.

"You need to come to the Pine Tree about four o'clock," Adele said to me. "I'm joining Chet and Tucker for an early dinner. I'd like you there too."

This was encouraging. "So, you aren't buying Tucker as the long-lost grandson?"

"I didn't say that, Ana. But I'd like a little more evidence. Will you come?"

"Sure," I heard myself say. "Meanwhile, how can I find out more about paddling in the swamp?"

"Go talk to Charlie Dixon. He kayaks everywhere."

I knew this was true. The proprietor of the Cherry Hill Pharmacy was an expert kayaker. Now that his wife was no longer in the picture, he could be seen with one of his several expensive slim vessels atop his car almost every evening. He probably knew every navigable inch of the local lakes and rivers.

"Thanks," I said.

"Grab one of the sandwiches and a drink from Max on your way out," Adele said. "That will hold you till later. Tell him it's on me."

10

Cherry Hill Pharmacy was only two blocks away, west past the City Park, and the day was warming. I wandered into the park and sat at a picnic table to eat my sandwich. Cherry Hill was sleepy but not on its death bed. Three years ago, we'd almost lost the drug store when Charlie was accused of murder. But now, the store was doing better than ever.

Shagway, the next town west, was in bad shape. About the only shopping you could do there was at a Dollar Store. Emily City, to the east, was much larger, but it was a longer drive than most people wanted to make. I smiled at my good fortune in finding a town that was small and comfy but healthy and adequate for my needs. Cherry Hill seemed to suit me perfectly.

I tossed my sandwich wrapper into a trash can and began walking the perimeter of the park, sipping my pop.

The Petite Sauble River ran along the north edge of the park. On the northwest corner, where the water ran beneath Mill Street, it was channeled into a stone sluiceway. This was the former raceway of a shingle mill, Cherry Hill's first business. Lots of bad memories for me were associated with the bridge on Mill Street. But that was also where Jimmie's mother, Dee, had found her courage and freedom, so it wasn't all bad. I turned east along the river. Here, the water was wide and fairly slow moving. A line of orange floats on a nylon rope stretched across the water. "Danger, Keep Out" and "Fast Moving Water" signs were posted between the floats and Mill Street. However, above the floats was a wide beach. Several canoes rested, keel up, on the well-worn grass. They were chained to a post with a notice that they could be rented by the hour at the City Hall. I looked farther upstream and saw the river flowing placidly between two frame buildings that faced Balsam Street.

City Hall was just north of my location, across the river, attached to the police station. I headed in that direction.

Entering the chilly block building, I approached an information desk.

"How does one go about renting a canoe?" I asked.

A woman I'd seen around town but whose name I didn't recall said, "Hi, Ms. Raven. You can take care of that right here."

"I'm sorry, I don't remember your name," I apologized. "But actually, I'd just like some information. Please, call me Ana."

"Oh, OK," she said. "There's no reason you should know me really, but I live over near Dee Ward, Jimmie Mosher's mom. My daughter plays with Beth and Lindsey. I'm Yvonne Michelson."

Now I knew where I'd seen her. Beth and Lindsey were Jimmie's half sisters. They all lived in a cozy home on north Dogwood Street that Habitat for Humanity had rejuvenated for them.

I smiled. "Thanks for the reminder. Can you tell me if any canoes have been rented yet this season? And how far do people paddle in an hour?"

Yvonne smiled back. "I can't give you names, but I don't see any problem with giving you some general info."

"Fair enough."

"There were a lot of rentals over the holiday weekend. Most people just putter around a bit. It's safer below the raceway.

"But the canoes are in the park," I protested. "People carry them all that way?"

"We have more rentals down there, including a pedal boat. The river widens into a little pond, you know. Kids can play in the water."

Actually, I didn't know that. How could I still be finding out new things about Cherry Hill after five years of living here?

"Did anyone rent for a long time? Say three or more hours?"

Tara scanned a piece of paper she'd pulled from a drawer. "Nope. Longest was two hours. That was a family group with about seven kids."

Not likely they had anything to do with me. As an afterthought I asked, "Do you rent canoes or kayaks out overnight?"

"We don't have kayaks at all. They'd probably be popular, but the village hasn't been able to afford any yet. And, no, nothing overnight. Everything has to be checked back in before five in the afternoon. We open at ten."

"Thanks, Yvonne. I'll have to visit that pond sometime soon."

I left my pop can in the recycle bin by the door and headed for the drug store.

"Hi, Charlie," I called as I walked down the long straight aisle toward the back of the narrow store. It was no surprise to find Charlie there behind the prescription counter. He was as dedicated to Cherry Hill as Adele. And he wasn't being distracted by an old flame.

"Ana! What can I do for you today, my friend?"

"Do you have time for a few questions?" I asked.

"Anything for you!" His eyes crinkled in delight. He swiped a hand over his bald head as if he were smoothing hair he no longer had, pushed the papers he was studying off to the side, and gave me his full attention.

Well, I had helped save his bacon. And his business. I was sure that contributed to his attitude.

I explained to him about my evening visitor or visitors and the stolen kayak.

"So, how long would it take someone to paddle as far as my property from either the mouth of the Thorpe or upstream from town?" I asked.

"Well, I'm not sure, but your mysterious paddlers probably didn't come from either of those places."

"No?"

"There are lots of two-track roads leading to the water that can still be driven, north of the river, in Thousand Lakes State Forest. Private inholdings too. I've used a few of them myself. But they can be rough. That's why I bought a four-wheel drive last year. Maps mostly don't show them, but I know a few good places where it's easy enough to put in."

"Places that might be close to my property?"

"Oh, sure. The thing is, the river gets so convoluted in there–backwaters, channels changing after big storms, downed trees–I'm not sure how anyone would be able to find your place, specifically."

I thought a minute. "Do you know how to get to my property by water?"

"Maybe. I think I saw your new cabin once last year, but it was probably by chance. I mean, if you just continue downstream you eventually end up in town, so if I hadn't managed to get back to my vehicle I could have just asked my brother to drive me back to pick up my Subaru later."

"Is that what you did?"

He thought a minute. "Well, I did have to call on Cubby one Sunday, but I think the day I saw your place I made it back to the car."

"Have you been on the river this year?"

"No. It's early yet. Sometimes college kids will clean up stretches. You know, cut out the dead limbs and drag brush back. But they usually wait till the spring high water has gone down. You don't want to get caught in a strainer."

I scrunched up my face. "A strainer?"

"The outside bend of a curve erodes, a tree's roots wash loose, and it falls across the river. But that's also where the current is strongest. On the outside. Your kayak can get pushed sideways into the tree and sucked downward. People die in strainers."

"Uh. OK, thanks for the lesson. I guess I need to be careful. If I get my kayak back."

"You should be fine, even now, if you don't get out into the main channel of the river. Otherwise, wait till later in June when the water is down. I'll give you a lesson on how to paddle around strainers if you want. I have a couple of extra kayaks."

"That will be great!"

"What kind is yours."

"It's a red Old Town Otter."

"Gees-oh-Pete, Ana! There must be a million of those. But if I see one floating loose, I'll grab it."

11

I spent the bulk of the afternoon poking around the pond west and downstream of the mill race. It filled an entire block, and I couldn't imagine why I'd never noticed it before. A screen of trees and bushes hid the open water from Cherry Street, so that was probably why I had thought it was simply a vacant lot. Cora and Jerry lived on Cherry Street, and I'd driven that route plenty of times. I even walked back to City Hall and rented the paddle boat for an hour. I'd never tried one before, and although tiring, it was fun.

Thinking during the time on the water didn't enlighten me as to who might be paddling in Dead Mule Swamp, or why. After an hour in the sun, the only things I was sure of was that I was getting my first sunburn of the season, and that I shouldn't have worn jeans.

I stopped by the drugstore again and picked up a jar of aloe lotion for my smarting skin then headed for the Pine Tree and the ladies room. When I had finished the rest room tasks, I slid into a booth. Jack Panther sat down across from me.

"You're beet red," he laughed.

I pulled my mouth to the side. "OK, don't rub it in, just because you don't burn."

Jack's Native American heritage gave him a skin tone that didn't broil under the sun.

He chuckled.

Jack had completely remodeled the moldering diner a few years ago when he came into a windfall pile of cash due to his genetics. The whole town was better for it.

"What do you think of that guy with the sun tan and all the gold?" Jack asked.

I gulped the ice water Jack had brought with him to the table. "Chester or Tucker? Well, Chester is the one who wears the gold. But they both seem pretty phony to me."

"Not like they are from around here, that's for sure."

"Tucker was raised in Hawaii. We haven't heard much about Chester yet, but he's certainly from somewhere with more sun, or else he spends money in tanning salons. I'm meeting them and Adele here for dinner. Feel free to eavesdrop whenever it's not too obvious." I grinned.

"Adele is falling for that guy, I'm afraid," Jack said.

I shrugged. "It's her life. But I sure want to know more about him before I encourage it. How about some coffee?" I asked, draining the water glass.

***

In about half an hour, Adele entered the diner, and I waved her over.

She eased into the bench across from me.

"Tell me how you know Chester," I immediately asked.

"I met him in college," Adele said. Then she looked up, and her face brightened.

So I wasn't going to get any private info right now.

"Yoo hoo. Over here," she called in a high voice, wiggling her fingers. She'd painted her nails! I'd never seen Adele act coy, and I didn't care for the look.

Chester and Tucker arrived together. Tonight, Tucker was wearing a down jacket over a t-shirt. He'd switched to long cargo pants and looked much warmer. However, I noticed he was still wearing sandals. Chester, in pleated off-white slacks and a light blue shirt, exuded style and smelled of Acqua Di Gio. In short, he reeked of money. If he was after Adele's savings, he was making a serious investment to pull it off. He sat beside Adele, leaving Tucker to me. The young man was carrying a lumpy plastic grocery bag. He stuffed it between us. Greetings were exchanged, and Chet gave Adele's shoulders a squeeze.

Jack had faded back into the kitchen, and a young waitress whose name I didn't know brought menus and took drink orders.

I'd hardly ever eaten dinner here, so we all spent a few minutes studying the plastic-coated cards.

I ordered a plate of pasta shells with red sauce and a side of broccoli. The men chose the meatloaf special, and Adele selected a dinner salad. Wow! She was usually a hearty eater. Was she trying to slim down for Chester? This was getting more serious by the minute.

Finally, the last plate had been removed, and we were all sipping coffee. So far, the conversation had been limited to small talk.

Tucker reached down and pulled out the plastic bag he'd brought with him. He set it on the table. "I have a few more items from my childhood that I thought you'd like to see."

"I want to see anything you've got," Chester assured him. "I'm all ears to learn more about the missing years. Darn shame I missed out on them."

"Well, I missed knowing you too, Chet. But I didn't even know my father, so how could I know you?"

The young man dumped the contents of the bag. The most compelling item was a bright green Beanie Baby frog. I recognized it as the toy in the snapshot Tucker had brought last time.

"So this is your stuffed animal?" I asked, picking it up. It looked suitably shabby to have been the possession of a toddler rather than a collector's item. The paper TY tag was gone, but the fabric tab between the frog's legs was still attached. I looked at it, but there were no markings other than the faded fiber info. I suppose that would have been too good to be true, to find his name, "Tucker S.," hand printed in indelible ink.

"His name is Legs," Tucker said. "I looked him up. They were all named Legs, and I guess my mom didn't suggest anything more creative. I remember carrying him all over the place."

An item of baby clothing had also been in the bag. It was a well-worn onesie with a yellow giraffe on the front.

"Yours as well, I assume," I said

"Yes, I guess it was a gift from Lyle. Mom had saved it in a box with this card." He slipped a hand inside the garment and pulled out a small square of cardboard, printed with another yellow giraffe.

There was handwriting on the card. "Love from Daddy."

Tucker pushed it across the table toward Chet.

Chet bent his head and nodded. "That certainly looks like Lyle's handwriting."

There was a short pause in the conversation. Chemistry between Chet and Tucker was happening.

Adele broke in. "What's in the book? More pictures?"

"Yes," Tucker said, pushing the small album toward Chet. "I'm sorry, I don't have any others with Lyle... my father. But at least you can see a few of me growing up."

Chester picked up the book. It was one of those small square albums that hold snapshots in plastic sleeves. He flipped through a few, studied them and passed the book to Adele.

Adele looked at a picture, then at Tucker, and then back at the picture. "You were a cute little boy. No question about that."

My turn was next. "Where were these taken?"

"Hawaii. We lived in Hawi, it's a small town on the big island."

"Did you always live there?" I asked, turning pages.

"I'm told my mom moved there when I was about two. I don't remember. A lot of artists went there after the sugar plantations failed. She was a potter."

I wasn't giving up. "Why did you come back to the mainland? What made you want to find your father's family?"

Tucker squirmed. "Mom got sick. Pancreatic cancer. She knew she didn't have long, and she told me about Lyle. I'd never heard anything about him before."

"And what did you do after that?"

"Came to California. It was where Mom said Lyle lived. After searching around Los Angeles for a couple of years, I stumbled onto his death certificate, and..."

Chester went pale beneath his tan. His mug clattered to the table, slopping coffee across the polished surface.

"Lyle's dead?"

I jumped up, grabbed a handful of paper napkins and tossed them into the spreading puddle.

Adele slid the photo album and the onesie a safe distance away and patted Chet on the back.

Tucker reached to rescue his frog.

12

"That's a helluva way to break that kind of news," Chester blustered.

"I assumed you knew," Tucker replied.

Chester calmed down enough to sit back, but his hands were still shaking. "Can you prove he's dead?"

Tucker thought a minute. "Not right now. I didn't pay for a copy of the death certificate. Maybe I can have one mailed. Sorry."

"Well, Lyle and I hadn't been getting along for a quite a few years, but he was my only child. This is somewhat hard to take in."

Tucker looked down and fiddled with the plush green frog.

I thought he seemed oddly indifferent to Lyle, but as he had pointed out, he never really knew the man.

Adele managed to get the conversation moving. "Tucker, after you found out about your father, what did you do next?"

Tucker looked relieved. "Um...right...anyway, that was a dead end. Ooh, bad pun. So I ordered one of those DNA kits, and that's how I found Chet. They match you up with near relatives if the other person gives permission."

I raised an eyebrow in Chester's direction.

"Yes, I had one done a while back. It said I was a mixture of Brit and Solomon Island stock. No surprises there. My great-grandfather sailed on the HMS Curacoa. Spent a lot of time in the South Pacific. Probably brought home a bride. Anyway, I lost interest. History bores me except for the stuff about my name."

He shook his head slowly and looked sideways. His eyes were moist. "I can hardly fathom that I have a grandson, and that he's located me."

I tried not to roll my eyes. At least one of these two characters was a phony. Or had I become so used to the transparency of country living that I didn't like them because they were different?

"Come up to my apartment for a nightcap, Tucker," Chet invited. Then he looked at Adele. "Well, let me escort this lovely lady home first."

Adele put a hand on his arm. "I'm fine, dear. I make it home alone every single day. "I'll have another cup of coffee with Ana."

Dear? I had to talk to Adele. And it sounded as if she wanted to talk to me.

After the guys had left, Jack himself brought us coffee refills.

"I hope that flashy man left money to pay for your meals," he said.

Adele looked chagrined. "Well, no. I guess Chester was too flustered after finding out that his son has died."

"Some gentlemen they are," Jack commented, leaving us with a carafe of decaf and carrying away the pile of wet napkins.

Although I hadn't had time to think about who was paying the tab, this conversation had been a bit much. I stared at Adele and plunged right into the issue.

"Don't you think it's just a little fishy, the two of them showing up here days apart? I'm worried about how involved you seem to be getting."

"Oh, Chester is all right. I know him, Ana. He'll give me money to cover dinner. And he seems to feel fine about Tucker. You worry too much."

I sighed. "Tell me about Chester."

Adele smiled and rearranged her bulk in the booth, reminding me of a nesting hen.

"As I said earlier, we met at college. Fullerton."

"In California? You were in California?"

"I'm a California girl," Adele confessed. "I grew up there."

This was almost more than I could process. I thought Adele had always lived here in Cherry Hill. "But, but... how did you meet Henry and end up here?"

"Fullerton had a great horticulture program. Still does. Henry was interested in expanding his father's store, growing organic produce before it was trendy. Henry's brother lived in Anaheim, so he lived with his cousins and attended college out west."

"And Chet was also a student there?"

"He was. We dated off and on, steady for a while. But then I met Henry, and, well... But Chet is a really nice man."

"You know his background? Maybe he's changed in forty years. Adele, I'm afraid he might be trying to weasel you out of your savings."

Adele looked at me in horror. "My little nest egg? Fiddlesticks! His family has a ton of money– big time fruit growers. That's why he's so upset with Eva. That girl would run through an inheritance in a flash, and she's not society material. She's turned into a latter-day hippie, and I think she's on drugs. But I am a little concerned about this boy."

"So am I!"

But Adele wasn't through defending her friend. "Chet's wife died quite a few years ago, he's estranged from Lyle, and he's disinherited Eva. No wonder he's so desperately hoping for some remnant of a blood line. And now Lyle is dead."

Another idea came to me. "Do you think Tucker might have stolen my kayak? Probably everyone from Hawaii knows how to paddle some sort of canoe."

"What on earth for? He doesn't seem like the outdoor type to me despite the way he dresses."

"Well, assuming you know Chet as well as you think you do, Tucker is the only new person in town. Most all of us already own a canoe or kayak."

Adele scrunched up her face. "I've heard about several break-ins. Aho's outbuilding, your cabin, a lady who lives north of me on the edge of town reported her yard shed was jimmied open and her lawnmower taken. It does seem like this is a larger number of petty thefts than usual. Still, I think it's probably not significant."

"Let's go," I said. "This discussion reminds me that I want to repair my cabin lock yet today."

Adele picked up the check and clucked her tongue. "I'm sure Chet will reimburse me."

"I sure hope you're right about him."

13

I headed home with a foam container of the pasta I hadn't been able to finish at dinner. I wasn't optimistic that Chet would ultimately pay Adele back. Thanks to Roger, I was certain I had more money than she did, despite her assurances of a nest egg. I probably should have picked up the tab.

The long evenings were a delight, and I took my time collecting some tools and the bag of hardware I'd purchased in the morning. Perhaps if I dawdled until almost sunset, the singer would appear, and I could catch him.

Nesting season was at its height, and I loved hearing the trills of the orioles as I strolled down the path to my cabin, pushing a wheelbarrow filled with tools and hardware. The two new boards for jambs were balanced and bungeed across the top. Cardinals whistled, and a vesper sparrow sang sweetly. A flash of orange in the trees confirmed my identification of the oriole's song.

Once I reached the cabin, I began making enough noise that birds and wildlife kept their distance. I'm pretty handy, and it wasn't a big job to replace the splintered jambs. I did have to saw the boards to length by hand since I had chosen not to run power to the cabin. By eight o'clock, I'd screwed a new hasp in place and was about to click the hefty padlock through the shackle and leave when I changed my mind.

I rummaged through the one box of supplies that was stored in the cabin and found a waterproof container of matches. Why not enjoy the first campfire of the season? Chad and I had fashioned a couple of rough benches from logs and slab wood and placed them around a rock-rimmed fire pit. Officer Harvey Brown had taken away the shovel, but a rake had been stored inside, and last year's dead leaves were easily cleared away from the area. I filled a bucket from the river and placed it nearby, just in case. Before very long, a bright fire burned through the gathering dusk.

I sat there thinking about Chester and Adele, wondering if he could possibly be good for her. It didn't seem so, but perhaps I just didn't want to think she might give up the store and go back to California. Tucker was a complete enigma. What did he want? Could he have found out through his research that his grandfather had money, or did he genuinely long for a family connection? I thought about my own son, Chad, who had done most of the work on this cabin. He was job hunting all over the country. Who knew when I'd see him again? He kept in touch fairly regularly, but had no roots here. Roger and I had divorced after Chad had started college. He visited me occasionally, but this was not his home.

The light continued to fade. Neither the singer, nor anyone else, was seen or heard. I'd probably warned them off with my fire. I was getting thirsty, and since I hadn't remembered the flashlight, I didn't want to wait until full dark to head back to the house.

However, the sky didn't seem to be getting any darker, and before long I realized there was a nearly full moon hanging above the trees. It would be a perfect, spooky setting for the ghostly singer to appear, but he didn't. I continued to sit quietly, taking in the gentle gurgling of the river where it flowed through one of those much-discussed deadfalls. A barred owl called "Who? Who? Who cooks for you?"

From a distance, a shrill whinny startled me into attention. My heart raced. Then I chuckled at myself; it was only a little screech owl. In a few seconds, its mate answered. Well, it was spring and the owls were happy. Why should I care if Adele and Chet were happy, too?

I sighed, rose, and put out the fire. I returned the bucket and rake to the cabin and locked the door. The wheelbarrow was already packed. I pushed it home by the light of the moon.

***

The next morning, I called the Sheriff's Department and asked for Harvey. The primary detective, Dennis Milford, and I do not get along well, and I really hoped Harvey was on duty. He was.

"Good morning, Ana! How can I help you? Has someone been on your property again?"

"Hi, Harvey. I don't think so, but thanks for checking. I fixed the door and put on a new hasp last night. I stayed out there till after dark, but didn't see or hear anyone. I'm calling to see if you were able to do anything with the shovel."

"Oh, sure. We lifted some prints, but they aren't on file. I do have yours, because of that trouble a couple of years ago..."

I sighed. Being involved in local mysteries was a mixed blessing. "I know."

"But that means I could eliminate you. Someone else left them."

"How long do fingerprints last? I mean, my son certainly used that shovel last year."

Harvey asked for clarification, "But the shovel was outside all winter?"

"Apparently. I didn't take it out this spring."

"Then it's highly likely these are fresh prints. They weren't preserved in soft paint or grease or polyurethane or anything. Just normal latent prints."

"OK. Thanks. Let me know if anything new turns up."

Harvey chuckled. "I can do that within limits."

"I know, but your office is supposed to supply me with crime reports for the newspaper. I heard there have been several break-ins lately."

Harvey answered in a crisp voice, "Yes, ma'am!" Then he laughed. "You'll get your report today. I do believe we usually send it on Thursdays."

"You do."

"But you're right. There seems to be a rash of petty thefts from small isolated buildings. I'll personally make sure the report gets emailed."

I thanked Harvey and hung up.

14

I needed some help to find my singer and my kayak. Keeping track of the school calendar was not on my radar, but I drove to town and pulled to a stop in front of 714 N. Dogwood Street, where Jimmie Mosher lived with his mother, Dee Ward, and his half sisters, Lindsey and Beth.

My question about the school year was pretty much answered when the girls burst out of the front door, dressed in play clothes, and ran to my car.

"Ana, did you come to visit us?"

"Will you teach us to sew this summer?"

"We'd like to get a pony."

"Jimmie said we can try making chocolate soufflé. It's hard."

"But we can eat all the ones that don't turn out."

"And the ones that do!"

They both dissolved into giggles. Lindsey was ten and Beth was almost twelve. They seemed to enjoy helping their brother in his culinary activities, although Jimmie was the one obsessed with becoming a restaurant owner and chef.

I exited my car and each girl grabbed one hand. They began dragging me toward the house.

Beth said, "Mom's at work, but she thinks we are old enough to stay at home without her this summer. Last year, we had to spend the days at Mrs. Grunder's house."

"We called her 'Mrs. Grumper' when she couldn't hear us," Beth said, giggling again.

"Most of the time, Jimmie is here anyway. And he's practically a grown-up," Lindsey added.

Indeed, Jimmie had been practically a grown-up since I'd met him when he was eleven. Taking care of his mother and sisters had been his priority for at least the past four years. And I had to admit that he'd done a remarkably good job without becoming an overly-sober teenager.

Once inside, Jimmie yelled from the kitchen, "Who is it?"

"It's Ana," the girls called in unison.

Jimmie appeared in the doorway, brushing floured hands on a baker's apron.

"Hi Ana! I'm trying to get the hang of homemade bagels. They'll be a great addition to our catering menu, and I can make 'em ahead and freeze 'em."

I shook my head in wonder. "Jimmie, you are just amazing! Do you ever take a break?"

"Oh sure. I only mess around in the kitchen when I feel like it. Except when we have an actual job."

I followed him into the kitchen and marveled at the amount of food he'd been able to prepare in this small space. The fragrance of hot raisins and cinnamon filled the room.

As if he could read my thoughts, Jimmie said, "We're almost at the limit of what we can legally sell in a year from a house. We'll either have to expand and upgrade this to a commercial kitchen or somehow buy back the Cherry Blossom."

"Jimmie! That building is a mess. I know you love it because your father established the restaurant, but how could you ever get it restored to a condition to cook there?"

He cocked his head. "Well, it's not as bad as you think. There's some water damage, but you know I've kept working at cleaning it up."

I did know this. He'd been doing it on the sly since before our adventure with Charlie the druggist had come to a conclusion in the decrepit building.

"Now, the realtor knows I spend time there. Of course, if someone else buys it, I lose it all, but so far I've only cleaned up. I haven't spent any money. Well, not much. And nobody's wanted it for over ten years."

"Sweat equity, for sure," I said.

Jimmie smiled. "Lots of it. She, the real-estate lady, made Mom sign a waiver that we are responsible if I get hurt or something. But Mom would rather have me there legally than sneaking around."

"I can understand that."

A buzzer sounded.

"The bagels are done. Come try one," Jimmie said, turning and heading for the stove. He pulled a tray from the oven, and the delicious odor became even headier.

Beth pushed a butter dish across the counter, and Lindsey opened the refrigerator and returned with a tub of cream cheese.

"We think he's got them just about perfect," Beth said.

I sliced a hot bagel, slathered butter on the porous surface, pulled off a piece and popped it in my mouth. I had to agree with Beth.

Jimmie moved the bagels that we didn't immediately eat to a cooling rack. "Did you just stop by to see what I had that was good to eat? He looked at me and grinned. He knew I was notorious for not having enough food in my house.

"Actually, I'd like to hire you to do a job if you're free."

"Are you giving a party?" Lindsey asked.

I shook my head. "I'm not. This has nothing to do with food."

"What, then? Can we help?" Beth wanted to know.

"Someone broke into my cabin and stole my kayak. I want to camp out there overnight, but maybe alone isn't such a good idea. I'd like Jimmie to stay with me."

"Us, too?" Lindsey pleaded.

Trying to break the negative response gently, I answered, "Not this time. We'll do it again with all of us when the weather is warmer and after we've figured out who my mysterious singer is."

They hadn't heard about the man who played music in my swamp, so I had to tell them all the details. Jimmie called Dee to make sure it was all right for him to be gone overnight, and we arranged for me to pick him up at about seven-thirty that evening.

***

Jimmie and I settled down in the cabin just at dusk, which was nearly ten o'clock now that we were in the same month as the summer solstice. We didn't want to attract attention, so we didn't build a fire. Since the cabin had no bunks or other amenities yet, we blew up air mattresses and covered up with warm blankets. The door was unlocked so we could make a fast exit if we heard anyone on the river.

Clouds had rolled in, and the night was not as bright as it had been on Tuesday. We visited in muted voices for a while. Jimmie just couldn't stop talking about the restaurant, but I didn't mind. Soon, we drifted off to sleep. Neither of us heard a thing all night.

15

It rained during the night, and the greenery shimmered with droplets of water in Friday's sunrise.

I delivered Jimmie to his house and was treated to another bagel. The girls were still sleeping. Dee was getting ready to leave for her job as a teller at the bank. She greeted me, asked how our adventure went, and approved Jimmie spending another night at my cabin.

Despite giving permission, Dee was frowning. "You'd better take a baseball bat or something out there with you. The girls told me about this man who's been on your property. Maybe the singing is just to lure you out there, so he can knock you out and rob your house."

It was possible, but she hadn't heard the depth of sadness that seemed to pour from the soul of the singer.

"That's probably a good idea," I admitted. After all, I had really no clue what was going on in the man's mind.

"The two of you are probably strong enough to overpower one other person, but I'd feel better if you had some kind of weapon."

"Don't worry, Mom. I'll take my Louisville Slugger tonight," Jimmie assured her.

Next, I dropped in at the police station. Cherry Hill had one officer and one desk man, in addition to Chief Jarvi. Tracy Jarvi was a tall, large-boned young woman who inspired confidence. No one ever questioned her ability to deal with lawbreakers.

The police station consisted of one big room in a gray block building attached, without consideration to architectural design, to the City Hall. The interior was dingy and cluttered. No one had thought to partition storage areas when it was built. I greeted Bob Clay, the man at the desk, who was busily keyboarding at a computer terminal. He looked up and nodded. But it was Tracy I had come to see, and he knew that without discussion.

She waved me over to her space, and we both sat down. "What can I do for you, Ana? Are you looking for some more information on the break-ins for the paper? I heard you've been a victim as well."

"True. My kayak is missing. It will be great to get your reports. There are enough instances that I'll use the topic for my next column, but I'm really here to ask you to check on something. Well, someone."

"How can I help?"

"I'm really concerned about Adele. You know, those two new guys in town."

Tracy nodded.

"She can vouch for the older one, that's Chester Alan Arthur Schoellkopf. But we don't know a thing about Tucker, the young man who claims to be Chester's grandson, except what he's telling us."

"Where is he from?"

"He says Hawaii. That looks believable based on his clothes and the tan. He's shown us some documents that make it look as if he's related to Chester, but I haven't asked to see his driver's license or anything. I didn't want to alienate him on our first meeting. And he is a carbon copy of Chester. That's impossible to deny."

"Well, I can't just randomly stop him and ask to see an ID either," Tracy said. "We may be a small town, but we aren't complete rednecks that dream up crazy reasons to question strangers. Has he broken any laws?"

"Not that I know of."

Tracy chuckled. "I can keep a subtle eye peeled to see if he runs the stop sign."

"Thanks. Say, what if I managed to get some things the two men have touched? Could you check their fingerprints and see if either one has a record? I suspect at least one of them is a con man."

Tracy shook her head. "We can't run them without probable cause for a crime. That's a violation of privacy. Now, if you can get a look at Tucker's driver's license, and it has a different name than what he's claiming, then I might be able to justify checking."

"What if I suspect one of them of breaking into my cabin? The Sheriff's Department lifted some prints from a shovel, but it's not coming back with any hits."

"Ana, you can't have it both ways. If those fingerprints aren't in the system, and either of the Schoellkopfs is running a con, it's probably not the first time. Their prints would bring up a hit."

What she said was true. So it probably wasn't one of them who had broken into my cabin. Or they'd never been caught at whatever it was they were up to. They? Were Chester and Tucker working together on some kind of confidence scheme? This was an interesting idea.

Tracy waited for me to continue. She was smiling patiently; I hoped it was only because she found my daydreaming amusing.

"Maybe I'll try to get their prints anyway."

"Don't do it. We can't use any evidence obtained that way, even if they are doing something illegal."

"But wouldn't it be helpful to know if one or both of them is on the level?" I was feeling a little bit desperate.

A sigh escaped Tracy's lips. "You are nothing if not persistent. Here's what I can do for you. I have a friend in Hawaii who's a private detective. Do you know which island Tucker is from?"

I thought a minute. "He said 'the big island.'"

"OK, that's the Island of Hawaii. That's where she is too. I'll give her a call and see if she can get some general background information on Tucker. Where's Chester from?"

"California. Adele knew him in college. He's legit, although who knows what he's up to. Cora thinks he's after Adele's money, but she claims his family has old money."

"Fortunes change. Who knows?" Tracy stood, and it was clear she'd gone as far out on a limb as she was going to, for now.

I rose, too.

Tracy concluded, "We'll keep our eyes open. But so far, they've been good for the town's finances. Chester is renting an apartment. They buy meals and sundries. If we were suspicious of every newcomer, we'd never keep the village afloat. Keep that in mind. I hate to sound negative, but Ana, maybe because of the crazy mysteries you've managed to solve you are trying to turn this situation into something more than what it is."

It was possible; no doubt about that. "Thanks," I said, and left. I wondered if I really was worrying too much. But I couldn't shake the bad vibes I sensed in the presence of the Schoellkopf men.

16

I stopped at Volger's Grocery to see if Adele was ready for her trip to Cold Rapids with Chester. If she wasn't, I thought we might be making a quick trip to Emily City to shop.

She told me she'd searched her closet and found a navy blue dress with some sequined trim she'd once bought for a party that ended up being cancelled. It was brand new.

"With some pearls and low heels, this will look nice both at a restaurant and for the concert."

"Will you be warm enough in the evening? I asked

"I'm taking that lovely cream-colored wrap Alice sent me last year. It's embroidered all over with flowers and leaves in a color almost the same as the fabric. I hardly ever get to wear it."

Alice was Adele's sister. She lived in Czechoslovakia, and I was sure the garment was a beautiful example of Slavic folk handiwork.

Adele was happy, and I hadn't been forced into the questionable role of fashion consultant.

***

The rest of the day was filled with chores around my house, but around eight in the evening I drove to town and picked up Jimmie. He sauntered confidently from his house to my old Jeep Cherokee with a solid wooden baseball bat resting on his shoulder.

Shadows were lengthening, but there was still over an hour of light left. Since the singer seemed to prefer dusk, or even full dark, I had decided it wasn't necessary to begin our watch any earlier.

As we pulled into my driveway, Jimmie asked, "Can we build a fire and roast some marshmallows or something?"

"I don't think that's a good idea. If the singer sees or smells anything, he isn't likely to come anywhere near us."

"Yeah, you're right," Jimmie said. "Too bad, that would be fun."

"We'll do this again, later, with the girls. After we've discovered whether this man is any kind of a threat."

"Do you really think he's trying to hurt you?"

For the umpteenth time, I considered this question. "I didn't think so at first. He certainly doesn't sound threatening. But then my kayak was stolen, and I know he was near my cabin when that happened. That doesn't seem so innocent."

Jimmie rolled the bat between his hands. "I see what you mean."

"But come in the house first. I did remember to buy some cookies. They won't be as good as yours, but they'll have to do. And I have milk." I grinned at my young friend.

He grinned back. "You're paying me. I'll eat anything you've got."

Jimmie was fifteen, thin as a toothpick, and I knew for a fact that promise could be literally true.

***

We settled down on the mats in the cabin, fully clothed, in case we needed to jump up and run outside quickly, at just about nine o'clock. It would have been nicer to sit outside and enjoy the colored light of sunset, but we had a job to do.

"Ana, can we talk?" Jimmie asked as the golden western window pane faded to silver and then gray.

"Sure, if we keep our voices down."

"You know me just about as well as anyone. Maybe even better than my mom," he whispered.

My heart did a somersault. "Well, I'm not sure about that, but what's on your mind?"

Jimmie shifted and raised himself up on one elbow. "Oh, Mom loves me. And I love her so much. She didn't give up when things were tough, and she stood up for me when it counted. And she got custody of Beth and Lindsey after we got the house in town. But she thinks buying back the Cherry Blossom is too expensive."

I was still thinking about his comment that I knew him better than his own mother. "Your mom hit a really rough patch and was betrayed by someone she thought she could trust. But she didn't care less about you then. She just didn't know how to make things better."

"Oh, I know that! I only mean that you've always had faith in me that I could make this restaurant dream come true. You understand how much I feel that connection with my dad, and Grandpa Jimmie. Because of your house."

He was referring to the fact that his grandfather, for whom he was named, grew up in the house I now owned. "You are a very determined young man. You were making your dreams come true when I met you, by any means possible at the time."

"We're trying to save as much of the money from the catering business as possible. Mom's job at the bank is enough to live on. And Wes, that's the girls' father, pays his child support most of the time."

"But your mom doesn't think the savings should go to buy a broken-down building?"

"No, that's not it. Not really. But we've only managed to save about eighteen-thousand dollars. We can't legally do too much business in one year out of the home kitchen."

"That's not very much compared to what the Cherry Blossom property is going to cost," I said.

"Right. The realtor has it listed at one-hundred ninety thousand. She says what we have isn't even enough for a down payment at most banks. There are three acres because of the parking and some open area in the rear. You know, that brushy field where the dirt lane comes off Tansy Road."

"They might come down a little on the price."

"Maybe. The owner is some guy who bought it as an investment when it went into the tax sale. It was ours, but

Mom didn't know about business stuff, and when she married Bert... well, you know."

I reached over and touched Jimmie's shoulder. "Yes, your mom wasn't in very good shape for a while there."

"Well, I could wish things were different, but they're not. Anyway, the realtor talked the owner into paying me a little bit every month to be a caretaker. Watch for vandalism, stuff like that."

I chuckled. Trust Jimmie to get someone to pay him for something he was going to do anyway. "That's great! But, your mom is right, you'll have to save a lot more to even convince a bank to give you a mortgage that large. And until you are eighteen, it would be against your mom's credit."

"Mr. Gorlowski came and looked at the building. He said the foundation and walls are still good, they're concrete block, but we'd..."

A deep voice floated through the still night air. "No-o-o-body, nobody knows the trouble I've seen..."

"Shhh," I hissed.

Simultaneously, Jimmie put his finger to his lips and quietly leaped to his feet. He sidled up to the window and took a quick look. Backing away he shook his head in the negative and pointed to the door.

Together we eased outside and hid on the upstream side of the cabin. The voice had been downstream.

We heard the crunch of a keel on dirt, but it didn't sound close enough to be in my clearing.

Jimmie peeked around the corner and shook his head again.

Chords of that unfamiliar instrument snuck between the trees. Echoes and the burble of the river distorted the pure notes.

Now, I also looked into the clearing. The music was other-worldly.

"...Oh Lord, I have so many trials, So many pains and woes."

"I'm going after him," Jimmie whispered.

I made motions like a batter getting ready for the pitch.

Jimmie nodded, reached inside the cabin and grabbed his bat.

The music grew in volume as the song brightened in emotional tone, "I'm asking for faith and comfort, Lord, help me to carry this load... I'm singing glory, glory, glory, Hallelujah!"

The sound of his footfalls covered by the louder music, Jimmie entered the woods downstream, and I quickly lost sight of him between the trees. I wasn't sure whether to stay put or follow him. I moved to the river's edge and peered down the dark waterway.

A clash of notes and a yell. I heard the scraping sound once more.

"Ana," Jimmie called. "Come quick!"

I ran through the woods. "Jimmie where are you? Are you all right?"

"I'm fine. Over here. By the water."

I followed his voice and found Jimmie staring down the river.

"I almost had him, but he jumped in a canoe and paddled away too fast."

"Who is it? Could you tell?"

"No, but it can't be either of the two guys you are watching."

"How can you be sure?"

"This was a black man."

17

Jimmie was too wound up to go to sleep. To be honest, I was too. It didn't seem likely that our dark singer would be back again this night, but we decided to stay in the cabin anyway. We talked about the man for a while.

"He was older. His hair was white and short. I could see it in the moonlight," Jimmie said.

"Could you tell what kind of instrument he was playing?"

"Nope, it wasn't anything I recognized. But he held it in one hand and pushed the canoe into the water with the other. Then he jumped right in and paddled off downstream."

"He can't be too old, then, if he's that agile."

Jimmie thought a minute. "Well, that's true, but Nana Cora is old and she gets around OK."

I had to smile. Cora was older than I am by a bit, but I knew she wouldn't care for the label of "old." That said, she was like a grandmother to Jimmie since she had been best friends with his grandfather. In fact she once told me they had been considered a couple until the older Jimmie hurt Cora's feelings so badly she could not forgive him. Although she was now happy with Jerry Caulfield, I suspected she always regretted losing her Jimmie.

Eventually, we both drifted off to sleep.

***

Saturday morning dawned crisp and bright. Through the window I could see a patchwork of new leaves glowing, still holding the magical yellow-green tints of spring. White shadbush in bloom twinkled through the greenery, as a light breeze caused small branches to sway. I hated to leave this lovely spot. However, the more than occasional appearance of the singer, and the thief–if these were not the same person–had shaken my sense of security. But I didn't have long to lie still and ponder this turn of events.

"Hey, Ana! I'm hungry."

We locked the cabin and walked to my house where I pulled out bacon and eggs.

"I'll cook. You make the toast," Jimmie instructed.

After we ate, I drove Jimmie back to town. He wanted to take the wheel, but Dee hadn't specifically designated me as an approved adult for him to drive with, so I said no. He was disappointed and said he'd ask his mom to talk to me about it.

I returned home. It was time to get busy and write my weekly crime column for the *Cherry Hill Herald*.

As much as I hated technology, I'd been forced to find a way to get on line from my house. I needed to be able to send and receive documents without driving to town. My basic smart phone had a hot spot connection. Well, it did if I could get a signal for the phone. It usually worked out here in the boonies, but not always. Today was a good day.

There was an email from the Sheriff's Department. It was a no-frills account of three break-ins. My own cabin, a vacation cottage along the Thorpe River, and a metal storage building on vacant property had been ransacked. The stolen items included my kayak, several small appliances, and tools. Other crime news included the DUI stops–just a normal number–mostly during early morning hours after the few bars in the county closed, and one domestic violence call with no one taken into custody. There wasn't much in the report that was interesting enough for a column.

The Cherry Hill Police had also sent me more information about the shed at Aho's Service Station. From that building, the items taken were also tools. The yard building belonging to a Ms. Karen Swick on Ross Street at the north end of town had a lawnmower stolen. This must be the lady Adele had mentioned.

All of these locations were remote. Ross Street was a short dead-end dirt road that was just barely inside the village limits. Aho's was at the very south end of Mill Street.

To me, this pattern suggested kids trying to make a few dollars by selling stolen items. I opened a blank document and began typing.

> A recent rash of break-ins scattered throughout Forest County should remind residents that although our area is relatively crime-free, it might be advisable to check on remote storage locations for signs of...

The phone rang. The land line. Everyone knew I preferred using that to my cell. I jumped up and ran to the kitchen where I snatched it off the cradle.

"Hello?"

It was Adele, and she did not sound happy. "Ana, I'm going to need you in town as soon as you can get here!"

I rolled my eyes. Adele's crises were many, and they didn't always need my immediate attention.

"What's up?"

"Chet's been arrested! There's a man dead in his apartment, and it looks like Chet shot him. Chet says he has no idea what he's doing here, and he wasn't dead after all, but now he is, and he didn't do it, and he found the gun, and Charlie called the police, and he says he heard the shot, and he can't figure out what to do, and he..."

"Adele!" I shouted at the phone. "Get a grip. You aren't making very much sense."

"But, Ana. They think Chet is a murderer, but he isn't."

"How do you know all this?"

Adele's voice ratcheted up a notch. "I know Chet wouldn't kill him even if they don't get along."

I sighed. "No, I mean how do you know all this information? When did this happen, and who's dead?"

"Just today. Maybe an hour ago. They let Chet make a phone call, and he called me because he doesn't know any local lawyers. I guess this means we aren't going to the concert. What are we going to do?"

18

I wasn't sure there was going to be any involvement on my part in trying to prove Chester innocent of whatever it was that had happened. However, I cared deeply for Adele, so I drove to town in hopes of calming her down. She really didn't have anyone else nearby who would support her on a personal level. Her daughter had moved away from our small town, and she rarely saw her grandchildren.

Adele had told me to come to her house. This fact alone indicated how rattled she was. It was the middle of the day, and she had left the store completely in the care of other people. Again. A few days ago it was because Chester was making her happy. Was he also making her promises he wouldn't keep? This time, he was causing her stress. I didn't think she needed either empty promises or extra grief.

Although it was a block out of my way, I drove past the grocery, planning to stop briefly to make sure things were in capable hands. Everything should have been fine. Adele had already arranged for Suzi Preston to keep the store open while she and Chester went on their date.

But the situation was worse than I imagined. The store was locked, the lights were out, and there was a hand-lettered sign taped to each entrance that read, "Closed for the rest of the day. Emergency. Open 8 a.m. Monday." Adele must have panicked and told Suzi not to come in. Since it was Saturday, this would give her a day and a half to get her emotions under control.

Five minutes later, I stepped out of my Jeep in Adele's driveway. She must have seen me coming, because she was standing on the top step holding the door of her enclosed porch partially open. She still wore her smock with "Volger's Grocery" embroidered on it.

"Oh, Ana! Thank you for coming. I'm so worried. Come in; come in."

We entered the living room. The coloring of her soft green walls and the pink-and-green flowered upholstery of the couch and chairs were usually calming, but the effect wasn't working today.

"Sit down, I've made us some tea." Adele pointed at the couch and scurried away toward the kitchen.

I found a comfortable position in one of the overstuffed chairs.

"So, what's going on?" I asked, once I'd sipped some of the strong black tea Adele brought. I set the mug carefully on a coaster on the end table.

"It's just crazy! Here's what Chet told me over the phone. They haven't let me see him yet."

"Go ahead."

Adele wiggled her behind and settled into the couch. "Chet was returning to his apartment after doing some shopping. He'd actually been getting groceries at my store. Oh! I hope someone took care of his milk. It's probably sitting on the floor of his living room."

"It's all right, Adele," I soothed. "It's evidence now. I'm sure Chester can afford a carton of milk. Keep going."

"Well, he was walking up the stairs. They're enclosed, you know, but the outside door at the bottom is usually unlocked. There was a little gun on one of the top steps. He couldn't figure out what it was doing there, so he picked it up."

I groaned. That had been a really stupid move on Chester's part, if he was telling the truth. "Then what?"

"His apartment door was open. I mean, not open, open, but unlocked. He thought that was odd. He's not from a small town, you know, and he was keeping that door locked. So he went in, and there was a man lying on the floor. He went over to look at him, and... Ana! you'll never believe who it was."

Shaking my head, and embracing the fact that everything about Chester became more unbelievable by the minute, I said, "Probably not, but try me. Did he call the EMTs from Emily City, or did our Fire Department guys transport him?"

"It was Lyle!"

"Chester's son?"

"Yes."

"What's he doing here? Tucker said he'd seen Lyle's death certificate."

"No one knows. He's dead! Well, he's dead now.

This was bizarre. "You're kidding me, right? Chester hasn't seen Lyle in years, and suddenly he shows up dead on the floor of his apartment, an apartment that is three-thousand miles away from where Chester lives, an apartment that was supposedly locked? Next you'll tell me that he was shot with the gun Chester found," I lifted my hands and made air quotes, "on the stairs."

Adele clasped her hands in front of her knees and rocked back and forth. "It's even worse than that."

"What could be worse?"

"Well, Charlie heard what must have been the shot that killed Lyle. But he didn't realize what it was. It was just a little popping sound. Then he got to thinking about it– how it couldn't have been a car backfiring because it was above the drugstore, not in the street– and he decided to go up and check."

"That should be good news. He can verify that the shot was fired before Lyle arrived. Your cash register receipts have a time stamp, right?"

Adele ignored my question. "Charlie scared Chet so much that he accidentally fired the gun when Charlie yelled at him to put it down."

My heart beat faster. "Oh, no! He didn't shoot Charlie, did he?"

Adele's eyes widened. "Heavens to Betsy, that would have been worse. No, Charlie's fine. The bullet just hit the wall. But now there's gunshot residue on Chet's hands, so he can't prove that he didn't fire the bullet that killed Lyle."

I thought a minute. "And the police can't prove that he did. Maybe he fired the gun in Charlie's presence to create a reason for the residue to be there."

Adele wailed and pulled the hem of her smock up to cover her face.

19

"How much do you really care about Chester?" I asked, moving to the couch and patting Adele on the back.

She wiped her eyes with the smock and turned toward me. Her features ware crumpled and sagging. She looked old.

"Are you going to be OK?"

Adele lifted her mug and gulped some tea. "Yes, of course. I just was so happy to see him after all these years. And to answer your question, I care quite a lot, but I'm not sure I want to give up my comfortable life for him. We did have something special, but that was forty years ago. He hasn't been here long enough for me to tell if he's still the same man."

"But you married Henry, not Chester, those forty years ago," I reminded her.

"You are right about that." Adele nodded. "No regrets. I was a California girl, but I enjoyed working. Henry offered me a settled life helping him with the family business. We would work together as equals. Chet wanted me to be a society wife... California style, not New York. But I just couldn't see myself in that role."

"And now?"

"Henry gave me everything he promised and more. We were very happy. But I have been lonely since he died. I don't know what Chet's intentions are. We've just been having fun together. I haven't pushed for more. And he hasn't pressured me. But I don't want him to take the blame for a murder he didn't commit."

"Adele, you don't know he didn't do it."

"Yes, I do," she answered stubbornly. "Let's go to the police station and see if they'll let us talk to him."

We drove back downtown and entered the plain block building. As usual, Bob was pounding away at his computer keyboard. Chester peered at us from the holding cell located at the rear of the room where he sat on a metal bunk. If his posture meant anything, he was dejected rather than belligerent. I couldn't recall ever seeing anyone in there before today. The biggest surprise was that Tucker was seated in the chair by Tracy's desk. He looked worried.

"Ana, Adele, good to see you," Tracy said, although she was using her formal police voice.

Chester stood and grabbed two of the bars. It was like watching a stereotyped bad movie of a small-town detention racket. He tried to shake the bars and snarled, "Get me out of here." Maybe he wasn't so dejected.

Adele came right to the point. "Is Chet under arrest?"

"At the present time we are holding him as a material witness, and possibly for his own protection."

"What does that mean?" Adele demanded.

"It means that we are waiting for a ballistics report, and that since the dead man, Lyle Schoellkopf, didn't belong in Chester's apartment and was shot there, Chester may have been the intended target."

Adele took a deep breath. "Chet was in my store very close to the time of the... incident. Ana pointed out to me that the time stamp on his receipt might clear him completely."

"We are certainly looking into all the evidence," Tracy replied in a even tone. Although we were all friends, she wasn't about to act unprofessionally when there was a murder to solve.

"We got a preliminary on the bullet," Bob called from the other side of the room. "It's a match for that gun. The little derringer."

"What about him?" I pointed at Tucker. "It seems like he'd have more reason to want Lyle dead than Chester did. After all, his new-found grandfather all but promised, in public no less, that he was going to make Tucker his new heir."

Tracy sighed. "We do have a problem with this one." She paused. "Meet Mr. Tucker Ian Metcalf."

I wasn't too surprised, but Adele's jaw dropped, and Chester leaned his forehead against the bars and moaned.

"So, you are a conniving little scumbag," Adele accused in a nasty voice.

Tucker didn't even flinch. "I am not. You'll see." But he didn't explain.

Tracy picked up the narrative. "I did ask my private investigator friend to look into the identity of a man named Tucker Schoellkopf. She easily found out that there is no such person, but she found records of a Tucker Metcalf that would be about the correct age."

"And here he is," I waved a hand in Tucker's direction. "Where was he when Lyle was shot? When was that, anyway?"

Tracy nodded and said, "Charlie heard what must have been the shot at about ten-thirty, but he's not sure of the exact time. We're trying to narrow it down. But he didn't go upstairs for several minutes, and he didn't look at a clock then, either. We got a call at eleven-oh-eight."

"When were you at the store?" I asked, looking at Chester.

"I was buying groceries at ten-thirty," he answered, sounding annoyed. "All this fine officer has to do is *look* at the receipt, and I'll be completely cleared."

Suddenly I realized one reason Chester looked more forlorn than usual. It wasn't only the stress of being accused of a crime. All his gold jewelry was missing. Probably he'd had to surrender it when Tracy had brought him in, although he was still wearing his own clothes. He would probably be totally irate if he'd been forced to put on an orange jumpsuit.

"Ten-thirty is an estimate of the time," Tracy reminded him. "I'm not sure I'm going into details with all of you. But I'm sure Charlie will be more than willing to tell everyone his story, so there's no point in trying to keep that confidential."

I looked back at Tucker. The young man looked way too smug. "So, again. Where was Tucker?"

Tracy sighed a second time. "He has been sitting right in that chair since a few minutes before ten. When I got the report that he wasn't using his correct name, I escorted him in for a chat as soon as I spotted him in town this morning."

20

Tucker tried to look innocent and angelic. His attempt only made him look sly. However, it was clear that he wasn't the guilty party. How fortunate for him that being caught out on one falsehood gave him an alibi for a major crime.

Probably Chester was afraid he wouldn't be let out of jail, that he might even be actually charged with the murder. He spoke rapidly, transferring information to us. "Don't look at me! It's not my gun. I never saw the thing before, and I had no idea Lyle was coming here. How on earth he found me, I'll never know. For that matter, how'd that kid find me, anyway?" He stuck a shaking finger through the bars and pointed at Tucker.

Tucker glared at Chester. "I'm your grandson, and I can prove it. The name problem is immaterial."

"You, you...cheap impostor," Chester sputtered. "You said Lyle was dead."

"I saw some paperwork, not a body." Tucker yelled, his face reddening.

"All right, all right," Tracy soothed. "For right now, we don't have quite enough to actually arrest you, Mr. Schoellkopf." She lifted a key ring from her desk and walked toward the bars. "This would be a lot simpler if you hadn't picked up that gun."

"That proves I'm innocent! Why would I get my fingerprints on it if I knew someone had just been killed with it?"

"That only works if you're telling the truth about it being on the stairs. And then firing it was extremely foolish," Tracy pointed out.

"That man scared me."

Tracy's temper appeared to be getting thin. "Yes, Charlie startled you. So you say. That was rather convenient for you. I am officially advising you not to leave town until we get this sorted out. Are you quite certain you were not the target?"

"Who'd want me dead? I haven't changed my will yet." His eyes flicked to Tucker and then focused once more on Tracy. "And I certainly won't be, now. You think the California Fruit Growers Charity Fund sent someone here to knock me off? Ha!" As Chester exited the cell he grabbed the lapels of his shirt and jerked on them to perk up the collar. "Where's my jewelry?"

Tracy shook her head in exasperation. "Bob will return your personal items, if you'll just step over to his desk. Also, you'll need to find somewhere else to stay. For now, the apartment is a crime scene."

"For how long?" Chester demanded.

"There's not much to process. Probably only one or two nights."

"And what about him? Maybe he's wearing makeup so he'll look more like me." He turned toward Tucker. "Check for a latex nose. Did you have to get a perm to make your hair curl like mine? Bleach it? What a faker."

Bob opened a locker and removed a paper bag.

Chester grabbed it. He briefly looked inside, turned to Adele and me, and said, "Let's get out of here."

He yanked open the door and motioned for us to lead the way.

As we left, I heard Tracy say once more, "Don't leave town. You are not officially cleared, either."

"Does that diner have take-out?" Chester asked as we stepped to the sidewalk. "I want to talk with you ladies, but not in public."

"Yes, of course they do. We can go to my place," Adele said. "In fact, you can stay with me. I have a spare room."

Adele and I both had cars in the parking lot. I didn't want to leave Chester alone with Adele, because I wanted to hear everything he had to say. "Let's ride together. I'll walk back to pick up my car later."

I opened the rear door of Adele's car and slid in, leaving the front seat open. That way I could watch the suspect, or whatever he was. Intended victim? Con man? Wrongfully accused martyr? Tucker's dupe?

Maybe I needn't have worried about Chester wanting to talk immediately. At any rate, he clammed up completely as we ordered sandwiches and fries to go. He headed for the rest room and while we waited for the food, he was combing his hair and restoring his gold to the appropriate locations.

Finally, we were seated around Adele's dining room table with the comforting scents of grilled hamburger and fried potatoes filling the air. I hadn't realized how hungry I really was. It was well past noon. The priority was the food, and we dug right in.

Chester was the first to wipe his mouth with a paper napkin and speak. "Adele, I know you have complete confidence in me. You've always been genuine. Even when you turned me down for Henry."

Adele actually blushed.

"Ana, I've heard that you are an excellent amateur sleuth, currently with the weight of being a crime reporter behind that talent."

"Well, the *Cherry Hill Herald* isn't exactly the big time," I said.

"Nevertheless, you've got the right to be asking questions. I'm hoping you'll help me prove my innocence."

I nodded, although reluctantly. "If I can help, I will. But, remember, I'll be looking for the truth. Wherever the evidence leads."

"You need a lawyer to be in your corner, no matter what things look like," Adele pointed out.

"I do. And I don't know anyone around here. I can call my lawyer in California to get a recommendation through her legal network, but maybe you know someone. I suppose I'd better let her know what's going on, in any event."

"We have one law firm in town, Fenwick and Case," Adele said. "J.R. does estates and wills. His partner is the go-to man for business contracts. I don't think they've had much practice with criminal cases. But I'm sure there are good lawyers in Emily City."

Chester finished off a can of Mountain Dew and wiped his lips again. "Your local guy will know who can do the job, though. Let's call him."

Adele went to get the phone book.

I unabashedly studied Chester Alan Arthur Schoellkopf. What was going on here? I certainly wouldn't need to manufacture enough words about petty theft to fill this week's crime column. This was hot news, but I did have to write the story soon.

21

"There's still time to go to the concert tonight, you know," Chester said just as Adele returned to the table.

"I'm not sure I'm up to it." She slumped into her chair.

"Why not? You already had your hair done. Looks nice. It would be a shame to waste that. We might have to skip dinner and just have some juice and sush afterwards. But we'll have to leave by five."

Adele had flipped to the correct page of the phone book, and she was dialing from her landline's handset. She appeared to be ignoring the request to keep their date.

I raised my eyebrows. "Soosh?"

Adele was speaking into the phone in low tones.

"You must know, even out here in the woods. Raw fish and rice and vegetable strips, rolled up," Chester explained.

"Ah! Sushi."

"It's California-speak," Adele said, handing the phone to Chester. "There was actually someone in the office, even though it's Saturday. I talked them into letting you have a few minutes with J.R Fenwick, himself. Be polite, Chet. Please don't tell him he practices 'out in the woods.'"

Chester stood and began speaking into the phone. He wandered into the kitchen. This apparent desire for privacy irked me. He was asking for our help, but he didn't want us to hear what he was saying to a lawyer? J.R. wasn't even his lawyer. Well, maybe I was reading too much into this. A simple request to find the correct person to contact wasn't a big deal. I decided I was just generally annoyed with Chester's attitude that we were all hicks.

"Why do you tolerate him making fun of Cherry Hill?" I whispered to Adele.

"He doesn't mean it. It's a very big shock to come here directly from southern California. Here he comes."

Chester returned with a glass of water. He'd finished the conversation, and set both the drink and the phone on the table. "He recommends someone named Walter Prince, in Emily City. But I won't be able to speak with him until Monday."

"I've heard good things about Mr. Prince," Adele agreed.

"So, I can't do more today, anyway. How about that concert? Let's go and forget about this nonsense," Chester urged, sipping the water.

"What about the tickets, though? Will the police let you into the apartment to get them?"

"I ordered on line. All I have to do is show them the email on my phone, and we pick them up at the box office. The problem is what to wear. These are the only clothes I have. For a couple of days, I guess."

"I don't have any of Henry's clothes left that you could borrow, and..."

He snapped his fingers.

"We'll leave right now. There's time to do a little shopping if we hurry. The concert doesn't start until eight."

"Oh, Chet, I'm not sure," Adele whimpered.

"For Pete's sake. I didn't kill Lyle, and as shocked as I am, he'd been out of my life for years. Even your police will figure it all out before long. Are you ready to go?"

"No, of course not. I have to change."

"Hustle," Chester demanded.

Adele shot me a pained look, stood, and headed for the stairs. "I'll try."

There I was, alone with Chester. I could have excused myself and walked downtown to my car, driven home, and ignored the man. But I couldn't quite let myself do that. Maybe I was turning into a reporter.

"Exactly how long has it been since you've seen Lyle alive?" I asked.

Chester rubbed his eyes and yawned. "Well, let me think. We had words when Eva ran off. That was... let me see... two-thousand eleven."

"One fight. You haven't spoken to him in five years because of one confrontation?"

"It was the culmination of a lot of disagreeable dialog."

"About Eva?"

"Yes. She was always headstrong, but Lyle supported her. Said she was going to be the CEO of a big company some day. He laughed when she talked back to him and told him she was going to do what she wanted to."

I wished I dared take notes, but decided I'd have to trust my memory.

"How old was Eva?"

"That's the thing. She was only sixteen. There's no way Lyle should have allowed her to take off with those bikers. He could have gotten law enforcement involved. Even in California they don't let sixteen-year-olds give consent for sex."

"You think she was raped?"

"Legally. I have no doubt she was agreeable, but the law says eighteen. She came home stoned out of her head more than once. That's just wrong."

I shifted uncomfortably in the chair. Taking advantage of minors was a different level of bad from confidence schemes. I felt Chester's pain. "And Lyle didn't want to do anything about it?"

Chester shook his head and looked down at the table. "It was so strange. It was as if Eva didn't matter to him." He glanced up at me with a startled look. "Maybe she didn't. Lyle knew he had a son in Hawaii. Even if he hadn't been in touch, he probably kept track of the boy. That snapshot with them together proves he knew of his existence."

"You didn't try to find Eva? You seem to be on the outs with her too. You've told us she's not in your will."

"She didn't want to be found. Sure, I tracked her down." He waved his hand vacantly. "But finding her location and finding *her* are two separate things."

"But, you've said she was just a kid. Maybe you should give her another chance. Do you know where she is now?"

Adele came down the stairs, smiling bravely.

Chester jumped to his feet at the sight of his college sweetheart, all dressed up. "You are stunning, my dear," he gushed.

The dark blue sequins on her dress sparkled, as did the beadwork on the beautiful off-white shawl. Adele had used just a bit of makeup, and I had to admit she looked extremely attractive. Silk and pearls beat a polyester store frock and a plastic name tag any day.

Adele took a deep breath, squared her shoulders and said, "Let's forget about all these crazy events for one evening. Things will get real enough tomorrow or Monday.

Chester held out his arm.

Adele stepped forward and took it, leaning into him slightly, "Oh, Chet! I don't want you to go to jail."

"I won't. Let's go, madame."

They did look happy together, although the stress was showing around the edges.

"Ana..." Adele began.

"Don't worry about me. I'll enjoy the walk to my car. You two go have a great time."

22

It felt like about a year since I'd had breakfast with Jimmie at my house. I was drained. But he and I had agreed to spend the night at the cabin once again.

I drove to his house, and his mother was home. Of course, rumors about the shooting had spread throughout town, and she wasn't feeling very positive about Jimmie possibly being in danger from some murderer who might be on the loose.

"Mom! Whoever killed that man can't be the guy paddling around in the swamp. The dead guy is a complete stranger. Nobody knows who it is. Somebody must have followed him to town to kill him. The singer knows his way around all those streams on the river. He's local. I'm sure of it."

Dee was less sure. "Ana, the last two times there has been some serious crime committed in Forest County, you've gotten my boy involved. I know he's a really competent young man, but..."

"Ana didn't get me involved," Jimmie protested. "I just happened to be at the Cherry Blossom when that lady went nuts. Ana rescued me. And we were all snowed in together at the Christmas party that went bad. You were there too. And the girls, remember?"

With a sigh, Dee threw up her hands in surrender. "The baseball bat, young man. Make sure you keep it close. I heard the police have the gun that man was shot with. Is this true, Ana?"

"It is," I replied. "I was in the Police Station when they confirmed it as the weapon."

"Then, unless this dangerous person has two guns, I suppose I don't have to worry about bullets flying around."

I reassured Dee as much as I could, repeating my theory that the singer didn't seem likely to be a dangerous person. After all, he had run away when Jimmie chased him the previous night. He probably wouldn't even appear today.

They invited me to eat with them. The take-out with Chester and Adele had filled me up, but I ate some salad, and Jimmie packed away enough food for both of us. He also boxed up some snacks for our evening munching.

On the way out of town, toward East South River Road and my house, I thought about the cold case that had been solved in "my" swamp. DuWayne Jefferson was probably out of jail by now. He might have a good reason to return to the riverbank, and he was a black man. Despite being incarcerated for several misdeeds, I thought of DuWayne as one of the "good guys." The man had saved my life.

"Jimmie, do you know Star and Sunny Leonard?" I asked.

"Sure. Well sort of. Star is older, but Sunny's a year behind me in school."

"Did you know that their dad went to jail on some old drug charges?"

Jimmie shook his head. "I only know who they are. I don't know their parents at all. I think they live way over on the east edge of the county. We don't ride the same bus or have any classes together. Star graduated a couple of years ago."

I was momentarily amazed that Star was out of high school. I hadn't kept in touch very well but hoped she had gone to the college of her choice.

"Well, I'm wondering if our singer could be DuWayne Jefferson, their father. His prison time should be done by now.

"You think he might be here to hunt you down? Did you send him to prison?"

Oh, no! He actually saved me from being stabbed by some drug dealers. He hadn't been involved in drugs for several years, but he did have to pay for his wrongdoing. And I'm pretty sure he was keeping watch on everything that was happening by paddling up and down the river."

"That makes some sense," Jimmie said. "I remember a little bit about that, but I was still in junior high. Mom was trying to get healthy enough to ask for custody of Beth and Lindsey, and I was really busy taking care of her."

My mind flooded with the events that had forced Jimmie to grow up very quickly. "Well, Sunny and Star's mother is dead. It was her remains that were found back by the river. The girls use their grandparents' last name instead of Jefferson."

"Wow!"

"I'm wondering if..."

"You think Mr. Jefferson is back there visiting where she was buried?"

"Maybe."

"Let's go look. Before it gets dark."

Jimmie and I made sure everything was in order at the cabin. Our blankets and mats had been locked in the building, so really, all we needed to do was stash some water and the treats. We made sure the air mattresses were fully inflated, and Jimmie grabbed the baseball bat. Soon we were walking more or less west toward where Angela Jefferson's skeletal remains had been found. I wasn't completely sure I'd recognize the exact spot. Of course, she'd been re-buried properly in a cemetery. I hadn't been to the location since.

At the time, all the vegetation had been trampled down by the investigators. It was sure to have grown back. After all, the discovery was four years ago. How was that even possible? As I was wool-gathering, we entered a small clearing with a cluster of white birch at one side, and I was jerked back to the present.

"This is it!" I said.

Jimmie swiveled his head, peering into the shrubbery around the edges. The river current gurgled placidly.

I checked the bank of the river, since this was another one of the places where it would be easy to pull a small boat out of the water.

There were no keel drag marks in the mud. Nothing appeared trampled. We found no footprints, no freshly broken branches, no teddy bears or beads or candles so common to impromptu shrines at places where people had died.

There was no evidence that any human had been here at all since that sad day four years in the past.

23

I suppose it was no big surprise that the singer did not make an appearance that night. We'd probably scared him away for good when we almost caught him. If he just wanted to paddle and sing there was plenty of river on which to cruise and croon. For that matter, there were abundant clearings along the waterway. There was no reason I could think of that he would prefer mine.

In fact, if it were DuWayne, wouldn't he have chosen to beach his canoe where Angela had been found rather than at my cabin? The whole thing made no sense.

***

In the morning, while Jimmie cooked breakfast, I phoned the home of Corliss "Len" Leonard, Sunny and Star's grandfather. The girls had lived with him for most of their lives.

The phone rang several times, and I pictured the older, slightly crippled man struggling out of his recliner to get to the phone. Then I laughed at myself. He probably had a cell phone.

"Hello?" It was Sunny. I recognized her voice right away.

"Hi, Sunny. This is Anastasia Raven. Do you remember me?"

"Miss Ana! How are you? I wondered if you forgot about us."

Guilt washed over me. We had promised to stay in touch. "I'm so sorry. I really have no excuse for not calling to talk with you more often. But today, I have a question I need to ask."

"It's OK, I've been busy with school and stuff. But now it's summer. Maybe we could do something together. Do you want to talk with my grandfather?"

"I'd really like to see you," I said. And I meant it. "Is Star home for vacation?"

"She's staying at college. She's trying to finish in three years instead of four, and she has a job. We got to see her for less than a week between semesters. She's so serious about everything."

So that gave me a basic answer to the question of whether Star had gone to college. I said, "We should get together and catch up. But, I do need to ask you a question. It might be an uncomfortable question. Maybe you'd rather I ask Len."

"Try me," Sunny said with a laugh. "I'm not a little kid anymore."

"Fair enough," I responded with a laugh of my own. "Sunny, I need to ask if your father is back in the area. Is he out of prison?"

"He's free. He's been out for almost two years. But we haven't seen him, either." She sighed. "Grownups make lots of promises they don't keep. He stayed in Chicago where he has friends."

Now I felt doubly guilty that I'd let Sunny and Star slip off my radar. "I'm really sad to hear that he hasn't kept in touch."

"Oh, he's not a complete deadbeat. He has a job, and he sends Grandpa a check every month. We just don't have a relationship. I get it; we were little when he left and now we're big. There's nothing there."

"You are a very wise young woman, although I'm sorry to hear that things didn't work out for you to know your dad better," I said. "How is your grandpa doing?"

Sunny's voice brightened. "His back isn't worse. In fact, they're talking about some surgery that might help him straighten up a bit and fix some of the pain."

"I'm glad to hear this!"

But Sunny was apparently still thinking about my other question. "Why did you want to know about my dad?"

There wasn't any good reason to withhold the truth. "There is a black man who has been canoeing past my property. He sings sad songs in a beautiful baritone voice, and he's stopped at my cabin a few times. But I don't know who it is. I only caught a glimpse of him once. I wondered if your dad might be coming to see where we found your mother."

"That can't be my father." Sunny was now actually giggling. "He can't carry a tune in a wheelbarrow. That's what Grandpa says, and he's right. I've heard Dad try to sing."

"I guess that answers that question."

"Who's making a racket in the background? Did you get a housemate? Oh! Did you get married?" Sunny's voice rose in pitch and volume on this last question.

I glanced at Jimmie and grinned. "Oh, no. I like my single life. Jimmie Mosher spent the night at my cabin. He's helping me catch the singer. Well, anyway, we hope to catch him and find out what he wants."

"Jimmie Mosher! I know him. He's so dope!"

"Is that good or bad?" Jimmie was skinny, pale, and possibly nerdy. I had no idea what other kids thought of him.

"Definitely good." Sunny giggled again. "Oh! Don't tell him I said that."

Laughing, I promised.

We chatted some more. I also learned that Paddy, the Irish setter, was happy and healthy. We made tentative plans to get together during the coming week. This time I would not let my young friend down.

It was Sunday morning, and I wanted to make it to town in time to attend church. I was happy being part of the small friendly congregation of worshipers at Crossroads Fellowship. Besides, Adele should be home from her date, and we could catch up. I knew she'd want to fill me in on the details.

Jimmie decided he wanted to go with me to church, so we made a quick stop at his house. Beth and Lindsey were tired of being left out of everything, and Dee decided she had been spending too many Sundays at home. Soon, I found myself sitting in a pew singing "How Great Is Our God," flanked by the three young people and their mother. It warmed my heart to be here with people I cared about, singing praises.

The mystery man's tunes had all had a spiritual message. Perhaps I should be watching for him at the churches in town.

I glanced toward Deputy Harvey Brown. He attended our church. But his hair hadn't gone gray. He couldn't be my singer. Maybe I should ask him if he had relatives nearby. A father or uncle, for example.

After the service ended, I expected to be accosted by Adele. That almost always happened. And we usually both helped serve the light refreshments that people enjoyed as they visited. But today, Adele was not to be found. Had she and Chester spent the night in Cold Rapids? Tracy had told Chester not to leave town. Would he be in trouble for going that far away? Maybe he was already back in jail.

I chatted with friends afterwards while nibbling on crackers and cheese and cookies. Dee's family had driven separately, and they honked and waved as they pulled out of the parking lot. Jimmie was at the wheel, grinning from ear to ear.

Cleanup was simple, since the refreshments hadn't required dirtying more than a few serving plates. I put away the remaining food, while Geri Longcore washed dishes. I wanted to avoid Geri. She would want to hear details about the shooting, and I didn't really know much when it came right down to it. I pilfered some extra crackers and cheese, jumped in my Jeep and drove to Adele's house to make sure she and Chester had returned safely.

There were two cars in the driveway and another parked at the curb. I pulled in behind that one, wondering what was going on. There were no emergency vehicles, though, so I assumed nothing truly awful was happening.

I knocked at the kitchen door, which opened directly from the driveway. Adele, wearing one of her church dresses, answered and pulled me inside. "Everyone is here," she whispered cryptically. "I'll pour you some coffee."

We walked through to the dining room. Chester and Tucker were seated on opposite sides of the table, fingering coffee mugs and not talking. There was a half-filled mug in front of the place beside Chester. Not wanting to align myself with Tucker whoever-he-was, I took the chair at the end of the table. Tucker was rotating his mug and taking an occasional sip of the contents. As the design on the mug was revealed between his fingers, I read "Love is family." I tweaked my lips at the irony, but didn't break the silence. Adele seemed to be taking a long time to pour coffee.

Speaking of irony, when she did appear, it was with my coffee in one hand, and a plate of crackers, cheese and cookies in the other. My lunch destiny for the day was determined.

Adele settled into the chair next to Chester, sandwiched some cheese between two crackers and clucked her tongue three times. "Where were we?" she asked, popping the savory snack in her mouth.

I suspected she knew exactly where the conversation had been suspended, but she was arranging the discussion to bring me up to date.

Chester took the lead. "Ana, it's nice of you to join us. Tucker, here, stopped by just as we were leaving for church. He's sticking with his story. Tell us again, in case we missed something."

Tucker sighed. His curly hair was matted in a few spots, and his shirt was rumpled. He looked ragged around the edges emotionally, but he lifted his head and began speaking. "It's pretty simple, like I told you. I was out of line to claim my last name is Schoellkopf. I admit it. However, it really is my name. I think. Maybe not. Lyle is my father. I guess Mom just put her own last name on the birth certificate. So, is that legally my name, or not? Wouldn't my father's name be correct? I don't know." He put his head in his hands.

Chester did not look ragged. He was wearing a nubby blue linen sport coat over his creamy shirt. His hair was combed. All his usual gold sparkled. Whatever else I might think of the man, he certainly looked like a million bucks. Maybe literally. What was he really worth? He stared at Tucker.

The younger man squirmed. "It just seemed so much simpler to tell you my name is Schoellkopf." He turned to me. "I've told them, and your police, that all you have to do is check in Hawi, and you'll find out my mother is…was who I said she is. She was a single mom, an artisan doing pottery, and…"

"It would just be a lot easier if we could speak with her to confirm your claim about Lyle," Adele said. "I'm sorry she died." Her tone did not convey condolence, only regret.

"What about the fact that you said Lyle was dead? Dead months ago." I asked. Certainly Tucker had lied about that.

"Like I said, I don't know what to tell you. They showed me a death certificate in Los Angeles County, California."

"We can easily check on the truth of that," I said.

"Do it," Tucker urged.

"Maybe Tracy already has," Adele speculated.

I was trying to process what we actually knew. I turned to face Chester. "Are you absolutely certain that the man who died in your apartment was your son, Lyle?"

"It certainly looked like him. But I didn't go through his pockets and check his driver's license." Chester shivered as if the mere thought of frisking a corpse was too creepy to contemplate.

"But you hadn't seen him in several years," Adele pointed out.

"Oh, be serious, Adele," Chester said. "Adults don't change that much. It looked like Lyle, The police are saying it was Lyle..."

I butted in. "Are they sure? I mean, has the body been officially identified? Either there are two Lyle Schoellkopfs, which seems absurd, or the death certificate is a fake or wrong, or the man at the funeral home isn't who we think he is. Well, that's convoluted, but you get my drift."

Tucker ran his fingers through his hair. "I've had enough, and I need a shower. I only tracked you down to try to clear the air, although you don't seem to believe I'm on the level. I don't know what else to do to convince you of who I am. The DNA test ought to be irrefutable. This other nonsense is all just one mix-up after another."

Chester took a breath as if to comment, but Tucker stood and continued his monologue, leaving no room for anyone else to speak.

"I'm going to go back to my motel and clean up. Your so-called police kept me all night until they could get confirmation of my identity from Hawaii. Seems like they could have released me as soon as they found out. There's five hours difference. If your inept hicks had called before they locked me up at four in the afternoon, it would have been eleven in the morning in Hawi. But no... they waited until this morning, and a Sunday to boot, to try to make contact. Thank goodness someone was on duty at six over there who was willing to check around and verify that I'm real."

Adele stood too.

Tucker shook his head and bolted for the door. "I'll see myself out."

Chester let out the breath he had been holding. "There is that DNA test."

25

I excused myself, as well. There was a crime column to write, and now there was a crime to write about. But I needed to get busy. Rehashing with my friends what we knew or thought about Tucker wasn't going to be productive.

Adele offered me crackers and cheese to take home, but I'd reached my quota of salty snacks for the day. Or so I thought.

Reaching my house, I rummaged through the refrigerator for something more substantial to eat. There was a partial bag of apples, some salami and bread. And eggs. But Jimmie and I had just had eggs for breakfast, with the last of the cheese, apparently. There were pretzels left in the box of snacks Jimmie had brought. Hadn't I just been shopping? I scrunched up one eye and thought about it. Tuesday. I bought groceries on Tuesday. Maybe I needed a freezer. Maybe I needed to get serious about remodeling this kitchen. Maybe I'd get organized enough to cook big pots of stew or pans of lasagna and freeze them in portions for moments such as this. Maybe. With a sigh, I folded a slice of salami into quarters and finished it off in two bites. I filled a bowl with pretzels, grabbed an apple, and headed for the tiny room I used as an office.

One perk of being a crime reporter was that Jerry had set me up with access to online archives of other newspapers. I began my research by trying to pull up articles about, and pictures of, Lyle Schoellkopf and Tucker Ian Metcalf.

The first thing I learned is that "Lyle Schoellkopf" wasn't as unusual a name as I'd imagined. The surname was German and meant "flat head," sometimes used as a nickname for a nitwit. That gave me a chuckle. There were lots of Schoellkopfs in the United States, and a small number of them had been named Lyle.

Since I hadn't seen the dead man, I didn't have much of an idea of the features I was looking for. Chester had said that Lyle looked more like his mother. However, I finally stumbled on the correct family line. Chester's father was a big-time fruit grower in California. Check. Chester had a son named Lyle. Check. The Los Angeles Times had a family photo featuring a young Chester posing with a smiling woman and a chubby boy of about ten whose hair was straight. The date was December 6, 1985. "The Chester Alan Arthur Schoellkopf family at Santa Monica Pier for the opening of the holiday festival."

The next picture was much more formal and in color. "Schoellkopf Orchards pass to son Chester after demise of founder Rudolf G. Schoellkopf." The pose was a middle-aged Chester standing in front of a life-size portrait of another blond, curly-haired man wearing a wide-lapelled business suit. Presumably Rudolf. The painting was reminiscent of British ancestral portraits, but the setting was pure California. What little of the house that could be seen around the edges of the figure was all cubes and glass and stainless steel. Beyond a strip of window at the edge, rows of green trees were visible.

And Tucker certainly completed the look-alike trio, although I could not find a single picture of a Tucker Metcalf from Hawaii. I tried "metcalf artisan potter hawi hawaii." Got a hit. Gloria Metcalf was listed as a maker of ceramics. I found a feature story about her work. She was known for her experimental glazes and asymmetrical tableware. "Nice stuff," I said aloud as I browsed through an archival catalog.

With her name, I was able to find an obituary. Just as Tucker had said, she moved to Hawaii from California in 1993, and had died this past year of pancreatic cancer. Check.

There was one blurry photo from a street fair with her booth front and center. A smiling, heavy woman held up an oval platter with one edge sensuously folded just the tiniest bit. The ceramics were nice, but beneath her lifted arm stood a small curly-haired boy. Check.

So, was it possible they were both telling the truth? Was everything completely above board, and my suspicions were based on nothing more than the fact that I didn't like the way they looked? Well, they both had insufferable attitudes against small towns. I didn't have to like that.

What I could not find was a picture of "our" Lyle as an adult. I found two other men by that name, both deceased.

Although it was Sunday, I knew that at least one of the members of our police force would be on call. Dialing the office would forward my phone call to that person. I got lucky; it was Tracy's day.

"Hey, it's Ana."

"Hey, yourself. I hope you don't have any new crimes for me."

We laughed.

"I'm hoping you can verify the identity of the man who was shot. I've been looking through newspaper morgues and can't find any pictures of Lyle, son of Chester Schoellkopf," I said.

"We did a basic search. His driver's license is valid. The picture is as good as DMV pictures ever are, but it looks like him, and the vitals match. We ran a background check. He's got no priors or fingerprints on file. Address in Marina Del Rey, California. Chet identified the body. You have some actual reason to suspect it's someone else?" I heard Tracy give a heavy sigh. She would not be thrilled to have to deal with a mis-identified body.

"No, not really," I said. "I just wanted to hear it from you."

"Consider it done."

"What about Mr. Metcalf?"

"No priors either. People in Hawi have known him all his life. He seems to have simply taken on the name of the man who was his biological father without checking on the legalities of doing so. He hasn't actually attempted to defraud anyone under an assumed name. Chester insisted Tucker has not tried to coerce him into transferring money or changing his will. I gave the boy a lecture about honesty and turned him loose after a night behind bars. He seemed duly impressed with the lack of amenities."

"So who do you think killed Lyle?"

"Off the record? Seriously, Ana. Off. The. Record."

"OK, OK."

"It's looking good for Chester, but we don't have a strong motive. Tucker might have done it in hopes of getting his grandfather's money. But he's one-hundred-percent out of the running. Right now we're pretty clueless."

"Thanks. I'll let you know if I stumble onto anything."

"You do that."

26

"Don't.. I'm not ready yet."
"Why did you do that?"
"This is getting out of control."

27

With a high-profile crime, one that happened right in town, and the perpetrator as yet a complete mystery, I had no trouble writing an interesting column for this week's *Cherry Hill Herald*, much more interesting than pilfered tools. When it was done, I hit the send button and, just like that, the file was on its way to Jerry. Maybe technology wasn't so bad.

I spent a little more time trying to find information about Lyle Schoellkopf, but the man was apparently as shy about the limelight as his father and grandfather, Chester and Rudolf, were welcoming of publicity.

It seemed pointless to watch for the singer any more. Jimmie had probably scared him off for good, chasing after him with a baseball bat. I was tired and discouraged.

I called Jimmie and told him we weren't spending any more nights at the cabin for a while. He didn't share my discouragement. He tried to talk me into working harder to catch the man. He even suggested tacking a note to a tree with a big red-markered greeting that someone on the river would see. Something like "To the Sad Singer," or "To the Bashful Baritone." It wasn't a totally crazy idea, but I was too tired to care. I told Jimmie I'd think about it.

While it was yet light outside, I fell into bed and remained unconscious until nine o'clock Monday morning.

***

The day passed quietly. I drank coffee from my favorite mug– the one with the drips of brown and blue glaze down the sides. I wondered if Gloria Metcalf would have liked it. I fried an egg with the last of the salami. I paid bills. I made a new grocery list, wondering as I scribbled what I'd forget this time. I sketched a floor plan for a remodeled kitchen, but didn't like the layout and threw the page in the trash. Mid-afternoon, I headed to town to actually buy the groceries on my list.

Adele was back at the store and seemed to be calmer. Routine is a comforting thing.

"Come eat dinner with us tonight," she urged. "Just me and Chet. We're avoiding Tucker."

I wasn't sure. "Do you think that's a good idea? Chester needs legal help, not anything I can offer. Or will this just be social?"

"He's got an appointment with Walter Prince, the lawyer J.R. recommended, this afternoon. You want to find out how that went, don't you? Besides, we need you to help us think this out."

The frozen items in my cart needed to be put away. My small refrigerator freezer would be packed. But this time I was purchasing enough ice cream, ready-to-heat dinners and pizza to last more than four days. And I had produce, shelf stable meals, and cans of vegetables and fruits. Bread was a problem. With all the other things I was buying, there was only room in the freezer for one loaf, but at least I shouldn't need to shop for more than a week. I felt so proud of myself.

Adele's voice penetrated my self-satisfied reverie. "How 'bout it?"

"Oh, sure," I heard myself say. "I need to go home and put this stuff away."

"Come at six-thirty. Chester is cooking, so the food will be ready as soon as I close up here."

***

Chester greeted me warmly at Adele's door. "Ana! I was informed that you'd be joining us."

The man looked more appealing than usual. He wore blue jeans and a black t-shirt with the AC-DC logo in gold letters. He had a plain butcher's apron tied around his waist. Since the bib was folded down, I suspected it was Adele's and was too short to fit him properly.

"You look cheerful," I said.

"Good news from the 'prince of lawyers.' Tell you while we eat." He winked.

"Smells great. What are we having?"

"Fish chowder– Bodega Bay style, hot rolls and a salad of oranges, onions and olives with homemade vinaigrette. I hope you don't mind cilantro."

"No problem," I answered, wondering if that was true.

"Can't get really good oranges this far from home, but it is what it is."

Car tires swished on the asphalt driveway, a door slammed, and Adele appeared.

Before long, we were filling up on the delicious food.

Coffee and coconut cream pie with mango sauce rounded out the meal. Adele pushed back her chair and began bustling about picking up plates and serving dishes.

"Leave them for later. I'll help," Chester offered.

Adele placed a pile of salad bowls on the corner of the table. "Well, we do want to hear about your meeting with Mr. Prince."

Chester took a slow sip of coffee and let out a sigh. "Aaahh. Fresh roasted beans. I had to go to Emily City to get them. This is good, if I do say so myself. Adele, we need to set up a gourmet coffee bar in your store."

His eyes were closed, so he didn't see Adele shoot me a nervous glance and shake her head.

Apparently restored to full energy, Chet began, "Mr. Prince doesn't think I have anything to worry about at the present time. The grocery store receipt may not cover the exact time of the shooting, which isn't able to be determined to the precise minute anyway, but it makes the timing very tight. Very tight, indeed. And, what would be my motive to kill my son? Even the lawyer couldn't imagine anything that sinister, despite my estrangement from Lyle. However, he has agreed to represent me should the need arise."

There was a knock on the front door.

"Who could that be?" Adele asked. "My friends all come in through the kitchen."

She rose and entered the enclosed porch. I heard the lock button turn and the door open. Then I heard Adele gasp.

Tracy Jarvi and patrolman Kyle Appledorn entered the dining room, with Adele trailing. Tracy and Kyle were wearing their formal faces, and full uniforms.

"Chester Schoellkopf, you are under arrest for the murder of Lyle Schoellkopf. Anything you say can be..."

I had no ability to focus on the rest of the Miranda warning, this was so unexpected.

"Sorry, sir, but we need to handcuff you. Please stand and turn around."

"But, why?" Adele wailed. "What has happened that you are doing this again?"

Chet rose, looking confused. "Is this because we went to Cold Rapids on Saturday? I assure you we returned the same day. Well, almost. It was after midnight. Is this the problem? Maybe there's some fine I need to pay?"

Tracy sighed as Kyle clipped the cuffs on Chester's wrists.

"I'm afraid you weren't entirely forthcoming with us, Mr. Schoellkopf. That little derringer belongs to you."

"Indeed, not!"

"Oh, yes, we traced the registration."

Chester continued to huff and deny ownership as they led him out the door.

Adele was stunned, but at the last moment she ran to the closet, grabbed a jacket and flung it over Chester's shoulders.

The plot and the chowder thickens, I thought. One verdict was certain. I do not care for cilantro, but the rest of the meal was delicious.

28

Adele and I silently loaded the dishwasher. My thoughts were uncharitable. Yet again, Chester had managed to get out of the work. I told myself that was unkind. After all, he had cooked an exquisite meal for us, and it wasn't his fault he was arrested. Well, if he had killed Lyle, it was his fault. At any rate, he had no control over the timing.

"Did Chester ever pay you for the meal at the Pine Tree?"

Adele flapped her hand dismissively and wiped at her face. A second tear plopped into the sink.

I tried a more pleasant topic. "Was the dinner and concert in Cold Rapids a good trip for you?"

Shuddering and mustering enough inner strength to stop crying, Adele gulped and nodded. I didn't attempt further conversation.

When we were finished cleaning up, I hugged Adele and drove home. As I pulled into the driveway, my cell phone rang.

"Hi Ana."

"Oh, hi, Jimmie. If you're calling to ask about tonight, I don't think we'll bother staying at the cabin for a while. I'll let you know if I hear the singer."

"You sound upset."

"Do I? Well, Chester has been arrested again." I was shocked to consider that Chester's arrest might be upsetting to me. I didn't like him, did I? He was so self-assured and cocky. And yet, he had taken Adele to a nice concert, and fixed us a wonderful dinner. "The police say the gun that was used to shoot Lyle belongs to him. To Chester."

"Wow! That does sound bad for him."

Abruptly, Jimmie switched topics. Like most teens, he was highly focused on his own activities. I could hardly expect him to feel much for a man he'd met only once.

"I did some poking around today."

"At the Cherry Blossom?"

"Gosh, no! I'm all in on your mystery man. I must have ridden my bike thirty miles. You know there are a bunch of old houses on the other side of the Thorpe River?"

"Sure. Well, I know about the big white one. There are more?"

"I checked at that one first, because it's right across the road from the river. It looks like there was a dock a long time ago, and maybe people used to go boating there."

That house loomed large in my memory. "I do know that one, pretty well, actually. It's where Sunny and Star's dad saved me from the drug gang. They were living there."

"OK, well, that probably explains why it's a little cleaner than the others. But nobody has been there recently, even though it's a good place for someone to get in and out of the river. The grass isn't trampled or anything, though."

I was trying to recall driving that road. It was now a dead-end at the river, at the canoe launch, across the water from the end of my own road. I had to drive for miles to get to that location which was less than half a mile from my house. I couldn't remember what else was there. "There are other houses?"

"There aren't any for miles and miles if you just go east. But, if you turn up Mulberry Hill, you know that really steep road that goes south, there are a couple more."

"OK. That's not exactly 'a bunch.'"

"Well, it's more than one. There's a really old place almost all the way at the top. It's caved in. I sure had a hard time riding all the way up that hill. It's super steep."

"Jimmie! You weren't exploring a ruined house all alone, were you? I know you think you're invincible, but that's dangerous."

Jimmie assured me that he was "very careful." We had a few words about his solo adventures, but I knew that with his history of independence, coupled with teenage confidence, it would be impossible to stop his exploring. My best shot was to temper an all-out expedition with some safety reminders.

"I'll be extra careful. For you. There was nothing to find at that place anyway. It's really just a couple piles of old rotting lumber. Looks like one was a little barn. No basement, either. I don't think anybody could even hide from the weather there unless they used tarps or something."

"Are you saving the best for last?"

"I am!" Jimmie's voice sparkled with excitement. "There's another house that's not as far up the hill. The paint is mostly gone, but it's still standing. I think someone has been living there."

Now I was afraid Jimmie would get in trouble for trespassing, even though I hadn't heard of anyone living on Mulberry Hill. "Maybe someone does live there. Somebody who doesn't want to be bothered. There are quite a few older people in Forest County who don't have enough money to keep their houses in good repair. Are there curtains in the windows?"

"Gosh. There were curtains. Sort of. But it's a dump compared to most houses. Do you really think it's somebody's home?"

I sighed. "We can find out easily enough, tomorrow. You might as well tell me what you saw."

"I looked in the windows. Some have real curtains, and some just have blankets tacked up."

"Poor people do that." I'd seen plenty of houses out in the country with beach towels and bedding for window treatments. It was sounding more and more like this house was being lived in permanently.

"I could see in one of the kitchen windows just a little bit. I don't know if someone lives there for real, but it's been used recently. There was a box of donuts on the table and coffee cups from a gas station. The door was locked."

"Jimmie! You didn't try to go in?"

"I thought it was an abandoned house and somebody was squatting. Anyway. I couldn't get in. Why would an abandoned house be locked?"

"That's my point. It's not abandoned. Stay away from there. We'll check at the City Hall tomorrow and see who owns the property and if the taxes have been paid."

"But that wouldn't mean the owner was living there," Jimmie protested.

"True enough. But someone in town will know if it's occupied."

"Mrs. Volger, or Nana Cora will know," Jimmie admitted. "They don't miss anything."

I grinned, even though I knew Jimmie couldn't see me. "That is the truth!" I put on my best adult voice. "No more adventures tonight, OK?"

"No more tonight. I'm too tired. I haven't ridden that far on my bicycle in a long time."

29

Sleep came slowly. Jimmie might be right– that someone was squatting at the house on Mulberry Hill. I couldn't remember hearing any history about that road, or who had lived there. I certainly hadn't heard anyone in town mention a resident out that way. Although my road no longer went through, I could cross the Thorpe River on foot via the old railroad bridge which was slightly south of the disconnected road. This person on Mulberry Hill would be a "country neighbor" of mine. Was the river such a barrier that I could have lived here five years and never known someone lived so close? Well, if they owned a car, they had to drive a very long way around to get to Cherry Hill. Maybe someone else brought them groceries. This made sense if it was an elderly person. The helper could even be coming from Emily City, making it less likely I would have heard anything about a resident. And Jimmie hadn't mentioned seeing a vehicle or tire tracks in the yard.

***

The phone woke me on Tuesday morning. I'm always groggy before coffee, but I snapped awake when the voice on the other end was Chester. Why would he call me? How could he call me?

"Ana. Good morning. I've already spoken to my lawyer, but your police department is being courteous and allowing me extra phone calls. Monitored, of course. In person. Low tech. The Chief is standing right here, and you're on speaker." The annoyance in his voice was obvious.

"OK, Chester. What's so important to tell me?"

"I've called Adele, as well. But I want you to look into this."

I sighed. "Into what?"

"The gun is mine. I've remembered when I purchased it."

This is convenient, I thought. Now that it's proven the gun is his, his memory clears up in that regard. I only said, "Tell me."

"They showed me the registration date, which was back in 1998. I bought the gun, but it was for my wife, Millie. She wanted something small to carry in her purse. It's a pearl-handled derringer. More of a toy than anything."

I butted in. "A lethal toy, since it was just used for a murder, don't you think?"

"Oh, well... yes. Anyway. I haven't seen the gun since then. Millie must have given it to Lyle. Which would mean he brought it with him to my apartment."

This actually sounded believable. Was I starting to trust this man? Then I thought about the scenario. "So, if Lyle brought the gun with him, he either committed suicide, or someone else took the gun away from him."

"Exactly!"

"Chester, suicide doesn't work if the gun was on the stairs, as you claim."

"It's the truth! It was on the step. I picked it up because it was so out of place. I had no idea there was a dead man in my apartment. Why would I make this up?"

"Don't be naive. If you killed him, you'd be certain to make up an alternative plausible story. The other choice is that if the gun was taken away from Lyle, the murderer would have to be strong enough to take him on."

"See, I knew you'd figure it out. Smart woman!"

"How do I know you aren't strong enough to do that? You look quite fit. Lyle was soft and flabby. All my initial instincts suggest that you could have taken the gun away easily. Tracy, are you listening?" I knew she was.

Her voice came over the line. "I'm here, Ana. You've come to the same conclusions we have. And, it's also possible that Mr. Schoellkopf, Chester, the one right here, has had the gun all along and is lying to us."

Chester put in. "Maybe he did kill himself. Maybe someone else moved the gun to the steps."

Tracy and I both laughed, which probably didn't help Chester feel more trusting.

"It's going to be pretty hard to sort this out," I speculated. "Both Millie and Lyle are dead, so they're not going to be able to verify or disagree with anything Chester says."

Tracy continued."That's certainly true. We're running the ballistics to see if the gun has been associated with any other crimes in the years since it was purchased. So far, nothing has turned up. But these kinds of searches can take a while. They aren't as high priority."

"You're keeping Chester in jail?" I asked.

"We are. He's the closest match for opportunity. We can't rule out that he was there at the correct time. He's linked to the gun. We just need a motive."

Chester blustered, "It could have been anyone! Someone could have followed Lyle here. Everyone seems to be coming here. I only wanted to reconnect with Adele, and suddenly Tucker shows up, and then Lyle. It's like a bad parade."

I thought back to Memorial Day, just over a week ago. I wondered if Chester had watched our cheerful small-town display with the same amount of disdain as his tone conveyed when he said "bad parade."

Chester continued, but now he sounded desperate. "What about that man who owns the apartment. How do you know he only heard the shot? Maybe he came up and killed Lyle. Adele told me he was mixed up in a murder before."

"Charlie Dixon? The pharmacist? You need to calm down and think about that," I replied. "He has no known connection to the gun, to you, or to Lyle."

Tracy again. "We've pretty much ruled him out, anyway. He was working on the computer, and Bob went over the data. Charlie saved the file he was editing several times between ten-thirty and eleven-o-eight, when he called us to report finding the body."

"But he could have run upstairs in only a few seconds!" Chester protested loudly. "If my grocery receipt marked ten-forty-one doesn't rule me out, then that man can't be eliminated because he saved a file a couple times. He was only a few feet away. I was three blocks away."

Tracy sighed again. "We're considering all the evidence. Despite your concerns, we aren't disconnected from modern law enforcement resources and basic logic. And, it's only two blocks from the grocery to the drugstore. Two, *very-small-town*, blocks, as you like to keep pointing out."

Chester's voice seemed farther away. "Someone must have seen me walking down the street." He was practically screeching now. "Give me that phone. I'm not done talking with my investigator."

"I think you are. We've been more than generous with your telephone privileges. Please remember that anything you say can be used against you, as well as to show your innocence. Ana, if you learn anything pertinent, you be sure to let me know."

"Absolutely," I said.

"Find out where Lyle has been since 2004," came through faintly with a tone of desperation.

The line went dead.

30

I needed coffee. I hated it when days began like this. It seemed as if all my friends were morning people, and that certainly would never be said of me.

Nobody who was known to have had the gun was alive except Chester. His wife and son were both dead. Who knew where that gun had been?

Maybe I could find out something about Lyle. The correct Lyle.

I called Cora and begged off helping at the museum.

However, it was too early to call California, but I got on line and started hunting for living people with that name. Internet databases would not have caught up with the fact that ours was dead. I didn't know a date of birth, but I could estimate it. The picture of Lyle as a child with Chester and Millie–Millicent? Mildred?–was taken in 1985, so he was probably born around 1975.

Using the *Herald's* account, I could get past all those blockades that kept non-paying users from seeing more information about people they wanted to research. I found one Lyle Schoellkopf born in 1974 and another in 1975.

The 1975 one was quickly ruled out. It showed him as being related to six other people, all in New Jersey. Also, judging from dates of birth, several of those were siblings, and Chester and Millie had only had the one child.

I had him!

> Lyle T. Schoellkopf, born March 5, 1974 in Pasadena, CA
> Related to Chester A.A. Schoellkopf and Emilia Leah Johnson (son)

Attended USC 1993-1994. No degree
1994-1995 no employment record
1995-2000 California Cartage
2000-present salesman for Triton Pacific
Current address 23745 Francis Street, Marina
Del Ray, CA.

"Emilia." Interesting that such a lyrical name would be forsaken for the mundane moniker, "Millie." But people have various tastes. Next I looked up Triton Pacific. With a name like that, the company could be anything. It turned out that while Lyle may not have wanted to take over as the family fruit grower, he hadn't strayed far from the tree, so to speak. Triton Pacific manufactured fruit processing equipment. Their web site boasted "we offer a full line of equipment solutions from slicers to peeling machines and more."

A salesman! That gave him all the leeway in the world to travel, meet women, turn up in odd places. Except maybe in Cherry Hill. Well, this was fruit country. He could have been here on vacation, or perhaps he was on a legitimate business trip in the general region. But how would he have known that his father was also in the area? For that matter, why did he want to see his father? Was he seeking a reconciliation? Maybe he had news about Eva he wanted her grandfather to know.

I tried to find out more about Eva. Maybe she had seen the gun, and could testify that her grandfather had or had not had it at some particular time. Her date of birth was February 24, 1995. After that, except for her parentage, there was no general information. I clicked on the correct links to check criminal records. Sure enough, she had a number of arrests on minor drug charges and some petty theft. However, it didn't look as if she'd done, or at any rate been caught, doing hard drugs, or dealing.

Time to call Triton Pacific, I thought. But a look at the clock told me it was only a few minutes past eleven. Only eight in California. It was unlikely there would be anyone in the offices yet, but I decided to try anyway. I went to the kitchen to get the landline phone from its charger cradle, but as soon as I picked it up, it rang. Caller ID informed me it was Adele. Another crisis?

"Hi, Adele, What's up?"

"Cora told me you were at home. Thankfully, there's nothing new."

I exhaled, realizing as I did so that I'd been holding my breath. "That's good to hear."

"I'm just concerned," she began.

That was code for "worried."

"Chet is counting on you to be able to find out why Lyle was in his apartment and to figure out who could have killed him."

That was a tall order. "I'm not sure we'll ever know why Lyle was here. Unless he confided in someone else, that knowledge died with him. Neither the police nor I can make much progress until we have a little more to work with."

"What's keeping you from looking? Why are you even home?"

"Adele! Give me a break. I just spent the morning trying to find out more about Lyle. It's still too early to call anyone in California. Why are you being so pushy?"

"He's innocent!"

"OK, I get that you believe that. But I hardly know the man. I have to start from scratch to get any useful information. Tracy will do ordinary things like interview Charlie and check the neighborhood. Maybe I can find out something by digging into their backgrounds."

Now Adele sighed. "You're right. I'm sorry, but I'm just so unnerved by it all. Come to my house after the store closes. I'll feed you. I have a box of things from college that can help you with background."

"All right. See you a little after six," I agreed.

After I ate a brunch consisting of a peanut butter sandwich and a salad, it was finally nine o'clock in California.

"Triton Pacific, how may I help you?" asked a crisp and cheerful female voice.

I'd already decided on my approach. "Yes, I'm calling from "Sunrise Packing Company." We'd like a reference on one of your salesmen." I paused as if checking the name. "A Lyle Schoellkopf, that's S-C-H..."

She cut me off. But politely. "You don't need to spell it. He works for us. But Sunrise Packing in Calexico? They don't do fruit."

Oops. I guessed if I was going to make up company names, I should check them first.

"No, we're in the Midwest. I'd like to confirm that he's here on a business trip."

"Let me transfer you to his supervisor." The receptionist now sounded more guarded.

In a couple of seconds, a male voice said, "Peter VanDyke, sales manager."

I had to think fast. "Mr. VanDyke. Good morning. I'm calling from Sunrise Packing Company. We're a startup, and we've received a call from a Lyle Schoellkopf who would like to meet with us concerning a used peeling machine. I'd just like to verify that he has the authority to sell previously owned equipment."

"Ah, Lyle's a good salesman. He's on an extended run to a number of our central state locations. Yes, certainly, we offer a nice selection of refurbished products."

"Thank you so much. Perhaps we'll be doing business in the future."

"Great! Where did you say you are located?"

"We're in..." I pushed the button to break the connection. Hopefully, he'd think the call was dropped.

31

After a tasty but pedestrian dinner, compared to what Chester had cooked, of grilled ham and cheese sandwiches and a salad of bland hothouse tomatoes drizzled with Italian dressing, Adele steered me in the direction of her living room. She carried a carafe of decaf coffee, and I brought two mugs. She settled herself comfortably in the deep couch, and I perched on the chair opposite. I poured the coffee.

"Come sit beside me," she said. "I want to show you this scrapbook." She leaned forward and patted an overstuffed album on the coffee table.

I moved over beside her, placing one of the mugs on a coaster, and she brought the bulging book into her lap. It was one of those with stiff pages striped with sticky lines and covered in a clear plastic that stuck loosely to the strips and held inserted items in place. These were easy to fill and maintain, but time had not been kind. The pages were yellowed, and as Adele flipped through, I could see that some of the plastic coverings had split.

"This is one thing I wanted to show you," Adele said, smoothing the plastic down across a spread of pages near the middle of the book.

"What am I looking at?" I asked.

Old square snapshots with the colors turning muddy showed a small room piled with cardboard boxes.

"My sophomore year, I found a studio apartment off campus and moved out of the dorm."

"OK. This is at Fullerton?"

"Yes. Chet and I had dated almost all my freshman year. We met at an orientation mixer." She turned the page.

A young couple smiled out from behind the plastic. The girl was trim, with sultry eyes, and wore low-riding jeans and a Fullerton t-shirt. Her hair was teased high, with curls hanging down by her ears. A man stood next to her, obviously older than she, obviously Chester. No one could miss that pointed chin and curly blond mop of hair.

I twisted to get a better look. "Adele! This is you?"

"Yes, indeed. I wasn't always stout. We asked the landlord to take this picture when he gave me the key."

"But Chester doesn't look like a college boy."

"He's older than I am. Maybe that's one reason I turned to Henry. And that's the point of this story." She put her finger on a photo which showed furniture in place and partially emptied boxes. In another snapshot, Chester was hanging a curio shelf on the wall.

"I get it. Chester helped you move into the apartment. And that makes him a hero. I don't want to dampen your appreciation, but boys help their girlfriends move all the time. It doesn't necessarily prove they are nice guys. I assume that's what you are trying to convince me of."

Adele huffed in annoyance. "Will you just listen? Chester and I weren't dating by then. I had spent a lot of the summer with Henry, learning about his dreams for the store back here. We weren't really a couple yet, but I had told Chester I didn't feel right going out with him. But Henry was busy the day I needed to move. Chester stepped in and helped me anyway. Jerks don't do nice things for the competition's girlfriend. He was, and is, a genuinely kind man."

"How can you be sure he hasn't changed? And, anyway, boys often have ulterior motives for being helpful."

"I just know, that's all. Chet was always a gentleman with me. I was a naive freshman, and he could have taken advantage of me in more ways than the common one, but he never did." Then she brightened and flipped back a few pages. "Look at some of the fun we had."

We were chuckling over pictures of a typical teenage beach party, complete with beer cans, a campfire, bikinis, and blue waves in the background, when my cell phone rang.

It was Jimmie. "Hi, Ana. I just wanted to let you know how I spent my day."

"Sure thing. I'm with Adele. Can she listen too? I'll put you on speaker."

"No problem."

I hit the correct button, and Adele said, "Hi Jimmie. How've you been?"

"I'm great, Mrs. Volger. I just wanted Ana to know that most of the cottages along the north side of the river aren't opened up for the summer yet."

"How did you find that out?" I asked, although I was pretty sure I knew the answer.

"My bicycle. I rode down all those back roads that go in to the river from the highway."

"Seriously?" Even though I knew how persistent Jimmie could be, I was surprised. "There must be a dozen or more of those old tracks through the woods."

"Nah, only about six that are very close to being across from your place. But a lot of them have forks and turnoffs near where they end that go to more than one summer place. Someone could have paddled from farther away, but those seemed like a good place to start."

"You said 'most of the cottages.' Some were opened for the season?"

"Well, maybe." Jimmie suddenly sounded a little cagey.

Adele spoke. "How can a cottage 'maybe' be open?"

"I just mean... I mean... sometimes it's hard to tell. You could see that someone had driven to one of them this spring. There were fresh tire tracks in the dried mud. I ran into a guy who was fishing. Maybe he came from one of the cottages."

"Did you talk to him?" I asked. "He might have seen our singer."

"No. I mean, yes, I did talk to him, but, well, I didn't think to ask him if he'd seen a guy in a canoe in the evenings."

"Did you know him? Does he own one of the cottages? I'm acquainted with most of the summer people because they come to town to shop." This from Adele.

"Uh, I don't think he's from around here. Maybe he was just fishing for the day. Hey, I gotta go. My mom is calling me."

"OK, Jimmie. Thanks for the report."

The line went dead, and I stared at the phone screen.

Adele made a guttural sound. "Fishing, my foot. Fish-y is more like it. I can tell when that boy is lying. He's no good at it. Now, what do you suppose he found that's such a secret he can't tell us?"

32

I turned to Adele. "Jimmie will tell us his secret in good time. Let's think about the Schoellkopfs. What if Tucker isn't Lyle's son?"

"Oh, that just seems more and more unlikely!"

"Unlikely that he is, or isn't?"

Adele gave me a funny look that I couldn't interpret. "He's probably Chet's grandson, don't you think? He's got the DNA test. He's explained using his mother's name, and it makes sense. The men are carbon copies, physically."

"I'm just not sure," I said, standing up and stretching. "I did some checking on Lyle this morning. He was working for a trucking company when Tucker was born, though, and then he became a salesman. Both of those occupations put him on the road a lot, so it doesn't rule out an extra relationship."

"There you go."

"So, you are good with Tucker being Chester's heir?" I asked. I was ready to head for home. I didn't want to argue with Adele, and I wasn't nearly so certain of Tucker's lineage as she appeared to be.

"It hurts my brain to try to figure out what else could be going on," Adele admitted.

"Maybe Tucker and your old friend are working some kind of con together. Maybe Tucker found Chester long ago and now they pull this routine on people to get sympathy. Maybe Lyle was working with them somehow, and they were infighting, and it got out of hand."

Adele pulled her mouth sideways. "Interesting idea. But what would that get them that's worth anything? Chester has enough money already. And their routine wouldn't involve killing someone—that's ridiculous."

"Maybe something went wrong with their standard plan. How can we find out what Chester is really worth? If he lost the family fortune somewhere along the way, then he's sure to be out looking for more money."

"Oh! And if he still has the Schoellkopf millions, then there's no motive for him to be involved." Adele was smiling now.

"All right. I think I can use the paper's credentials to run a background check on Chester. I can at least find out if he's been through any bankruptcies even if I can't get an exact statement of his worth."

"That's sensible," Adele said. "Just keep an open mind. You seem to dislike my friend just because he's not from here. But, Ana, only a few years ago, you weren't from here, either."

I sighed. "Point taken."

***

It was almost eight in the evening when I returned home, but not quite. That meant not quite five in California. Quickly, I searched on line for the phone number of the Vital Records Office in Los Angeles County and punched the number into my phone. A female voice answered with a bristly, "Yes." Even in that one word, I could tell she was not pleased to receive a call at 4:56 in the afternoon.

"I'm wondering if you can check the records for the death certificate of a Lyle Schoellkopf. It would have been in the last couple of years."

The voice sighed and rattled off a standard answer so fast I could barely understand her. "Are you a direct relative, authorized party—such as a member of law enforcement, an attorney representing the deceased's estate, or a funeral director acting on behalf of any of the above? If the answer is no, I cannot provide you with an authorized copy of a death certificate. For public records, apply in person, by mail, or check our website to file a request for an informational copy which will take up to twenty days to process."

"Uh... thank you," I stammered. "So you can't even tell me if someone has died?"

"Look, lady. It's quitting time. Check the obits on line. This is the information age, you know?"

The line went dead.

Now it was my turn to sigh. Of course. This didn't have to be so difficult. I typed "obituary lyle t schoellkopf los angeles" into my search box. No exact matches came up. I tried again with "california" instead of "los angeles." Still nothing. I had a brain wave and checked the Social Security database using the log in from the newspaper. This got me two deaths, but neither one was in California. Well, I already knew that sometimes it took as much as two years to update the records on the Social Security site.

But it wasn't looking good for Tucker's claim that he'd seen a death certificate. Not to mention that our Lyle had, in reality, been alive until a few days ago. Why would Tucker lie about Lyle being dead? Obviously, to get Chester to leave everything to him. If Tucker could get Chester to change his will, then kill Chester, and make it look natural, he could be gone with a fortune before anyone wised up. Chester's fortune... I was supposed to be checking on that.

I looked back through the notes I'd taken to remind myself of Chester's father's name. Rudolf. Probate Court records were public. After about an hour of intense research, I'd learned that the orchards and related businesses had been worth $2.1 million when it all passed to Chester in 1980. But what had happened since then? Real estate holdings showed Chester Schoellkopf as the owner of record for 227 acres of prime fruit-growing valley land. So, clearly he was still worth a bundle. But maybe he was cash poor.

Was there some reason he couldn't sell a portion of the property in order to flush out a bank account? Maybe the orchard had been left to Chester with some sort of strings attached. Was it possible that Chester was only allowed to glean income from the fruit-growing operation, but the land itself was in trust for a descendant?

If that was Lyle, then Chester might have wanted his son dead. That didn't help. If the trust was for the next generation, then the missing Eva, and now the newly-appearing Tucker stood to gain, not Chester.

33

Who besides Chester could have killed Lyle? There were only three strangers in town, and Chester was one of them. My mysterious twilight singer wasn't even identified yet. Was he somehow involved? The third was Tucker, but he had an airtight alibi since he was sitting in the police station when the murder occurred.

Could the time of death be wrong?

Maybe Chester had killed Lyle earlier and gone to the store, hoping someone would find the body while he was two blocks away. What if Lyle had actually been killed around ten in the morning? Even earlier?

No, that didn't work because Charlie had heard the first shot, and he'd actually seen Chester fire the second shot. Even if Chester and Tucker were pulling something as a team, someone would have had to fire the gun between 10:30 and 11:08 in a location close enough to the drugstore for Charlie to hear it.

Maybe I should talk to Charlie. Maybe I should ask Tracy just how accurately the time of death was established. Was it based on when the shot was heard or on other medical evidence? I wasn't even sure who did those kinds of tests in our rural county. Did we have our own Medical Examiner? I thought not. It was more likely we shared services with Sturgeon County which had a hospital. Had someone official come to Chester's apartment and made tests? Was Lyle taken to a morgue for an autopsy, or had the body just been transported to some funeral home? Were any tests performed right away, or was the evidence collected later, possibly hours later, when it would have been difficult to determine if the death occurred at 10:15 instead of 10:45.

And what about the singer? I had come to think of him as someone benign, someone who had no interest in harming anyone, a sad man who simply wanted to remain anonymous. But what if I was wrong?

If the singer was the killer... well, I didn't know a thing about him except that he was a black man who could play a musical instrument. The population of Forest County wasn't lily white, but news of anyone who was unfamiliar would spread through town like a rippling wave of fire. If that person had dark skin, he or she would be noticed even more. Of course, it was possible the singer wasn't a stranger to most people. I never had checked with Harvey Brown to see if he had any visiting relatives.

It was late, but I took a chance that Harvey might be working this shift. I picked up the phone. The person at the desk at the Sheriff's Office said Harvey was on patrol duty, but she would ask him to call me.

While I was in the kitchen scooping black cherry ice cream into a bowl, the phone rang. It was Harvey returning my call.

"What's up, Ana? Has your thief come around again?" he asked.

"No." There was a moment of dead silence and then I sighed. "Harvey, you may think I'm being ridiculous, or maybe even racist, but I need to ask you a question."

"Sure. I know you have no problem with the color of my skin."

"A few days after I reported my stolen kayak, and you checked the fingerprints on the shovel, Jimmie Mosher got a look at the singer. He was a black man with white hair."

"But he didn't recognize this man? He didn't know him?"

"Nope. I was, uh... wondering if you had any relatives visiting, or might know of anyone..."

Harvey gurgled out a deep belly laugh. "Oh, Ana... you don't have to be so coy. No one is currently visiting with my family. Of course, I can't speak for all the black families in the county, but you've learned how life in small towns is. Unless a person was intent on keeping a huge secret, everyone would quickly know who has company, who they are related to, and whether they have any roots here, or any valid business being here."

"And you don't know of any such person?"

"I don't." Harvey laughed again. "But I'll keep my ears open."

I thanked Harvey and hung up.

My final action of the evening was to write out a request for a copy of Rudolf's will– now public record through the probate court– and to look up the fax number of where the request should be sent. Zapping it westward would be my first errand of the next morning. I felt as if I'd taken in a lot of information this day, but that I was no closer to having solutions to the many puzzles.

34

I faxed the request for the will from the newspaper office the next morning. On the same trip, I stopped by the jail. I had no clue what the regulations were concerning visits with prisoners.

Tracy was breezy and magnanimous. "You can talk to Chet any time you like. No regular visiting hours because we don't often have inmates who stay long. The county takes care of any who are serving actual sentences locally. We did move him to the back so he has a bit more privacy than in this holding cell." She waved a hand toward the cage where Chester had been imprisoned the first time he'd been picked up. "The only thing is, you're not his lawyer, so no private conversations. I'll bring him to this cell and you can listen to him rant until he's blue and you're comatose if you want."

"Hopefully, I won't need to stay that long."

Tracy grinned. "You've got that right. I don't think I could outlast this bombast." She laughed at her unplanned poem.

In a couple of minutes, Chester, now wearing prison orange, had been transferred to the public cell at the back of the office room. He no longer looked defiant. In fact, I detected a hint of fear in his eyes despite his words.

"Ana! It's about time you showed up to do something for me. My lawyer isn't very optimistic about bail. It's that ridiculous gun. You have to prove I haven't seen it for years."

That seemed like a tall order. I pulled a lightly padded, no-nonsense metal chair closer to the bars and sat down. "It's really hard to prove a negative, you know. Can you give me any suggestions as to how to learn who did have it?"

"No."

"Oh, come on. You can do better than that. What are the choices? Millie must have given the gun to someone. Was she likely to give it to Lyle? What about Eva? If your granddaughter was in trouble so much, I wonder if she stole it and your wife never noticed it was missing."

"That girl! That's got to be the answer. Such a sneak thief. But I think she would have sold it for drug money." He stood behind the bars, clutching at them and staring intently down at me. Was he trying to be intimidating, or did it only seem that way as a result of our relative positions?

Refusing to feel cowed, I cocked my head and looked up at Chester. "That's a reasonable idea, but if she sold it, it's unlikely to have turned up here with Lyle's body."

Chester looked as if he were going to explode. "I can't help that! You want me to come up with ideas, but you don't like them when I do."

"Calm down. We're exploring possibilities. I'm not bashing your statements, just considering them. Choosing a likely lead is going to be much more productive than running after every thought. But, since we've brought up Eva, where do you think she is? It's going to be important to locate her. She and Lyle are certainly the two most likely people to have had the gun."

Chester's face distorted with loathing or, perhaps, rage. "I have no idea where the little tart is. And I don't want to know."

Clearly, he wasn't going to be much help in finding the girl. I tackled another subject. "Someone has to arrange Lyle's funeral. I'm sure that won't be Eva, but shouldn't she be notified? There must be something you know that will help locate her."

"Look, the last time I heard from her, she was living on some commune in Santa Barbara. They got busted for having a stash of serious weapons, and their founder was called up on drug charges. Sounds like your standard 'love, peace, happy dust' group, right?"

I glanced over at Tracy.

Tracy made a few notes on a memo pad and said, "Sure, I can see if she's still there. But that sounds like the nineteen-sixties, not the twenty-first century."

Chester waved a hand. "I know it. But anything goes in California. This bunch survived somehow, and they even made it past being caught far on the wrong side of the law. They're still there. Maybe Eva is too."

Chester may have been at odds with his family members, but he had a responsibility here. I reminded him, "Seriously, what are you planning to do about funeral arrangements."

"That lawyer, Prince–he's working it out. I talked with him this morning. He knows what has to be done. There won't be any service. No one would come anyway. The body just has to be shipped to California. He'll be buried in the family plot. There's plenty of room, but no hoopla."

All is forgiven in death, I guessed. Or most anyway–there was the "no hoopla" part. Chester's attitude seemed harsh. Maybe his coldness had contributed to Eva's attitude. I reminded myself that there are always two sides to every conflict. Maybe Eva had some good reasons for running away. "What about Lyle's wife? I don't remember you telling us about her."

"She left him years ago. Drat. I suppose we'll have to try to find her."

Tracy spoke up, but she didn't sound pleased. "What's her name? I can run a basic search. You should have mentioned her days ago. Are they still married? Perhaps she should be the one planning the funeral."

"Lyle said they were divorced. I have no reason to think that's not the case. It's Danielle something. Williams, Wilcox, Wilson? I can't recall her maiden name."

Tracy turned and began tapping at her keyboard. "Wilcox. Danielle Amber Wilcox Married February 14, 1994. Divorced July 18, 2004, Reno, Nevada. So, that's official. In that case, we're not obligated to notify her. But you should do it as a courtesy. It could affect her Social Security benefits."

"All right. Prince can take care of that too. I'm sure she has no interest in getting involved in our family again."

"Why did they divorce?" I asked.

"Why do you think it's so easy to believe Tucker is my grandson?" Chester snapped. "Lyle wasn't exactly discreet about how he spent time on the road. Tucker just pushes the timetable back a bit farther than we knew about."

35

Not much else was going to be accomplished with Chester right now. Tracy agreed to let me know if she got in touch with Danielle, or more importantly, if she got lucky and located Eva.

I decided to see if I could figure out what was up with Jimmie. He'd certainly sounded evasive on the phone the previous evening. I drove to the northwest side of town and found Beth and Lindsey standing near the corner of Dogwood and Susan Streets. I watched Beth toss a baseball in the air and then swing hard, sending the ball flying north along Dogwood. Jimmie was fielding, about a third of the way to the dirt turnaround at the end of the street. Their house was literally on the edge of town. It was one reason the property had been abandoned, and was available when Habitat for Humanity had stepped in to help Jimmie's family.

"Hey, Ana!" Jimmie yelled, reaching up to capture the fly ball in his glove. Since he was facing the length of Dogwood Street, he saw me coming. Beth and Lindsey whirled around. They all ran toward me.

"The great summer pastime," I teased.

"You're out," Jimmie said, playfully shoving Beth.

"Next time..." she countered.

Then they were all leaning in the windows of my car, greeting me and asking me if we could go swimming at Turtle Lake and have a picnic at the dam or maybe rent kayaks.

"Well, why not?" I thought. Out loud, I said, "Ask your mom. If she says yes, you've got a deal, as long as we can do a couple of errands too."

"Sure. Like what?" Lindsey asked innocently.

129

My face cracked into a grin. This was perfect, and I didn't even plan it. "Well, I need to talk to Nana Cora about something. Maybe we can kidnap her for a picnic. I'm not sure she would kayak."

Jimmie had pulled out a cell phone and was rapidly punching the screen with both thumbs.

"We have hot dogs in the kitchen," Beth said. "We were going to have them for lunch anyway. But it will be lots more fun at the lake, with you!"

"Hold on," Jimmie said. "Mom hasn't answered yet."

Lindsey stuck out her tongue. "You know she'll say yes. She doesn't really like it that we're here alone every day."

Beth grabbed her sister by the arm. "Let's go pack up some stuff. I'll do the food. There are more hotdogs in the freezer. You grab our swimsuits, and towels and stuff." They ran toward the house.

This was my chance to talk to Jimmie alone. "Was there something you wanted to tell me last night that you didn't want Adele to hear," I asked. "You sounded like you had a secret."

Jimmie reddened. With his fair skin, emotional responses were telegraphed to his face whether he liked it or not. The phone in his hand dinged. "That's Mom," he said, getting a temporary reprieve from answering my question.

Then I had a brain wave. It was more of a drive to pick her up, but maybe Sunny Leonard could join us for the picnic. It was still early in the day, and there was plenty of time.

"Mom says it's a great idea," Jimmie said.

"Good. Let's go inside and talk to your sisters. I just thought of something." We headed for the house.

Within thirty minutes it was all arranged. Beth and Lindsey were eager to have another girl join us, and Jimmie didn't object. Since Sunny was closer to his age, he probably felt they would have a lot in common. With the addition of Cora, that left him as the only male in the group, but he didn't seem bothered.

We had to choose between swimming and kayaking since the boat rental was miles from the swimming beach, and the young people agreed on swimming. I didn't have my suit with me, and my house was in the wrong direction, but it was fine. I was wearing shorts, and I could wade if I got too warm. And, the air was heating up– a fine day in June.

Cora agreed to the picnic. She said she'd walk home and change into shorts. We could pick her up there.

Once we were in the car, on the way to Cora's house on Cherry Street, Beth quizzed me. "What errands did you want to do, Ana? So far we haven't done anything except have fun."

"Well, I need to talk to Nana Cora. Now, we'll have lots of time for that. And, I'd like to drive past a house on Mulberry Hill. It's over on the same side of the Thorpe River as the dam." I looked at Jimmie.

He perked up. "You do believe me, then?"

I smiled. "We'll ask Cora who owns it. She'll know– probably without looking it up. We could go to the Register of Deeds office, but this is more fun."

"Tell us; tell us," the girls chorused. "What's the big mystery? Do we get to help solve it?"

"Maybe," I said. Your brother thinks someone is staying in a house that looks more like it's abandoned." I glanced in the rear view mirror to see their faces.

"A squatter!" Beth squealed, delighted.

"Someone dangerous?" Lindsey asked, squirming.

"Probably not much danger," I said. "I wouldn't take you there if I thought anyone was going to get hurt." But then I remembered the events of the past December. Maybe Lindsey had been a bit traumatized by the adventure at the Janes mansion. We pulled to a stop in front of Cora and Jerry's house.

When Cora slipped into the other front seat, I realized we had a problem. Legally, the car could only carry five people. I couldn't ask her to drive a separate vehicle; she had never gotten a driver's license.

36

"Um, this isn't going to work," I said. "We're out of seats, and we still have to pick up Sunny."

"Lindsey and I can share a seatbelt," Beth said.

Lindsey giggled. "Or I can squish behind the back seat. I'm little. It would be fun."

I thought about those options. Technically, it was illegal. Technically, would I be contributing to the delinquency of a minor? In reality, we'd be traveling for a few miles on dirt roads with almost no traffic. There was less than half a mile between the Leonard's trailer and a turn off the main highway. This was Forest County, not Cold Rapids. "You can share a seatbelt," I said.

Sunny was waiting for us at the end of her driveway. Her light brown face was animated, and she squealed and ran to the car when I pulled in. "Miss Ana! What fun! I'm so glad to see you."

"Hop in. The back will be a little crowded, but it's not a long drive."

There were casual introductions. Jimmie blushed when Sunny greeted him, and Cora said that all the students who worked at the museum called her Mrs. C, and Sunny could do that too.

I waited until I saw no cars at all coming down the road, then drove to the next corner and turned south onto a dirt road. We were home free. Probably.

Turtle Lake Dam was a popular recreation site on the Petite Sauble River. There were picnic tables and grills scattered around a grassy lawn. It had a swimming beach, changing

132

building, and a couple of pavilions. A hiking trail that crossed the dam was mowed and signed. The trail snaked into woods on the north side of the impounded water.

There were a couple of cars in the parking lot, but the area wasn't crowded. We grabbed our bags of food, charcoal, and disposable table settings and headed for a picnic table in the shade. Cora had brought a plastic tub with her. When I picked it up, it was cold.

"Cookies from the freezer," she explained.

"Yippie!" Lindsey yelled.

Cora was smiling broadly. "Oh, my. This brings back such wonderful memories."

"Like what, Nana?" Jimmie asked.

"Nana?" Sunny said, looking from Jimmie to Cora and back. "She's your grandmother?"

"Not really, but I feel as if we're related," Cora said. "And that's all part of the memories. When I was a girl, there was a group of us who lived along the river. We were all friends, but Jimmie Mosher, that's this Jimmie's grandfather, was my best friend. A boy named Laszlo lived in a house near Ana's. That house burned down years ago, and George and Ruby Harris lived nearby. We had such adventures!"

"That's cool," Sunny said.

"We often rode our bikes here to swim during the summer months. The pavilions weren't here then, but the beach and the float was. Now, don't let me slow you youngsters down. Go change!"

Cora and I got the charcoal lit, and we went to the lake, took off our shoes and waded out a short distance. I'd never seen Cora wear shorts, but she didn't seem self-conscious. Jimmie finished changing first, and he was already swimming for the raft before the girls appeared. The square floating platform had a low diving board and was anchored away from the shore.

The sisters were eager to play. Lindsey splashed Cora and me, and then Beth followed suit. Sunny was unsure if this behavior was acceptable, but since we hadn't scolded, she playfully slapped the water near me and grinned.

"I'm almost as tall as you are," she teased. "Bet I could win in a water fight now."

"OK, that was fun," I said, "but Mrs. C and I don't have any dry clothes. You don't want us to drip on the fire. Then we couldn't cook the hot dogs."

Cora and I headed for the grassy shore.

For the better part of an hour the kids splashed and chased each other, and they spent some time lying on the raft in the sun, talking and laughing. Cora watched them, but seemed to be lost in thoughts or memories.

When the hot dogs were cooked, I stood and waved. The youngsters swam back to shore.

After we'd stuffed ourselves with wieners and chips and topped it all off with chocolate chip cookies and lemonade, I said, "Shall we go explore Mulberry Hill?"

Cora shot me a look I couldn't interpret.

Everyone scrambled to clean up the remains of lunch and change out of their swimsuits. Soon we were again packed in the car.

"You ate too much," Beth told Lindsey. "You're wider now."

Lindsey wiggled her hips to take up even more space, and Sunny rolled her eyes. Then she looked sideways at Jimmie. He grinned in teenage camaraderie against the antics of the younger children. In truth, they were all pretty much toothpicks.

We continued west, and soon we turned left and began to climb Mulberry Hill.

"Remind me why we are we going here," Cora said.

Jimmie answered. "I think there's someone living in the house up here on the left. Ana said you would know who owns it."

Cora answered. "I know who used to own it. George and Ruby Harris, the friends I just told you about, grew up here."

Now it was my turn to pick Cora's brain. "Do you think the property is still in their family?"

"As far as I know. But it's been vacant a long time. Drive all the way up the hill if you would, Ana."

I continued to creep upwards. Cora kept trying to look past me, through the window on my side. We passed the old Harris house. Still no vehicle there, or any obvious sign of use. The hill was indeed steep, especially toward the top where there was an actual switchback curve. We reached the corner with Shagbark Road, and I turned around.

As we descended, Cora rolled down her window and craned her neck to look to the east after we were below the hairpin. "Oh my," she exclaimed. "It's fallen in."

"What, Nana?" Jimmie asked. "Did you know who lived there? It's just a bunch of fallen boards now."

"Mrs. Guinto from the Philippines, and her donkey, Koko." Cora got a faraway look in her eyes. "I wonder if I could find the little cemetery."

But before anyone could ask what she meant about a cemetery, we were at the house where Jimmie thought he'd found evidence of a squatter. I pulled to the side of the road. Something winked from a window. A reflection? Or was someone watching us?

37

"Let me go knock on the door, Ana," Jimmie asked. "I was here before– maybe the person saw me then, and will recognize me."

"Not on your life, young man," Cora said. "You don't know a thing about who's inside. Give me a minute."

She immediately began working her smart phone. Cora has always been better with technology than I am.

"What are you doing, Nana?" Beth asked.

"Checking the tax records. The museum account has access. Here we go. The taxes are up to date, and the owner is listed as Ruby Harris Henning. So the property is still in the Harris family.

There was a lot of squirming in the back seat that was making the car rock. I needed to make up my mind quickly as to exactly what we were going to do.

"All right, let's all go to the door together," I said. It didn't seem likely that anyone would feel threatened by two women and some kids.

The back doors opened.

"But stay behind Cora and me. We don't know..."

It was too late. Jimmie and the girls had tumbled out and were running toward the house.

"There are curtains, Ana," Beth yelled.

"Blankets," Jimmie corrected.

Jimmie was about to knock on the door of the house, and Cora was just getting out of the car when the door opened, and a tall black man with a cap of curly, short white hair stepped onto the stoop. He reached out and shook Jimmie's hand.

It looked to me as if Jimmie said something to the stranger. And they weren't acting like strangers at all.

The man turned and took in each of us. His eyes paused on Sunny as if he were studying her hard for some hint of recognition. After examining each of us, his gaze settled on Cora.

Nodding to her, he asked, "Cora Dubois?"

"George Harris," Cora answered, her tone almost reverent.

"I guess my secret is out," George said.

"I didn't tell them," Jimmie said. "Honest. Ana was just determined to find you, and she's good at that sort of thing."

George turned and put a hand on Jimmie's shoulder. "It's all right, son. After you found me yesterday, I knew I couldn't remain anonymous much longer. Come in, everyone."

We followed George Harris into his childhood home. The door opened directly into the kitchen. The appliances were missing, but a kitchen table and two moldy chairs sat in the middle of the room. A blue nylon jacket was draped over the back of one of them, and some crusty take-out boxes were open on the table. They bore the logo of a fast food chain located in Emily City. Empty water bottles had rolled to the floor, and a half-filled plastic-wrapped case of water rested beneath the table. A cooler had been shoved against the base of the peeling cupboards. A narrow wooden box with suitcase latches rested on a countertop. Except for the blankets at the windows, there were no other signs of occupancy.

Beth sniffed and wrinkled her nose, then covered her mouth, embarrassed.

"Ladies, why don't you take the chairs," George offered.

Until this time, we had all been still, silently processing this discovery. Now, that changed.

Cora and I settled into the chairs. The girls sat cross-legged on the floor, and Jimmie and George remained standing, leaning against the cabinets. General introductions were made.

George was surprised to learn that I was now the owner of the old Mosher farm.

"So, you are the George that used to play with Mrs. C?" Sunny asked.

"I am. And my sister Ruby and I also played with Jimmie's grandfather who was also named Jimmie. They look just alike." George grinned at young Jimmie. "I thought I was seeing a ghost when you talked to me yesterday. Laszlo Szep hung out with us too."

A vision of look-alike grandfather and possible grandson, Chester and Tucker, floated through my brain.

"Tell us some stories," Lindsey requested. "Nana hasn't told us about when she was a girl."

George, too, was confused by this pet name. He ignored Lindsey and said to Cora, "These are your grandchildren?"

"No," Cora answered. "You know Jimmie and I had a falling out in high school. But when I met the grandson, I felt as if he could have been mine. These two girls," she turned her hand in the direction of Beth and Lindsey, "are his half sisters. So these three call me 'Nana.' Sunny is a friend."

"Is your grandfather still alive?" George asked Jimmie.

Jimmie shook his head and looked at the cracking, faded linoleum on the floor.

Cora answered the difficult question. "Our friend Jimmie, his wife Sandra, and their son, Lee, this Jimmie's father, were all killed in a terrible car accident."

"I was in the car too, but I don't remember. I was just a baby," Jimmie said, not lifting his head.

There was an awkward pause in the conversation.

George stretched out a hand to the back of the chair where Cora was sitting. I thought perhaps he was going to pat her on the shoulder, but he grasped the chair to support himself. His knees buckled and he sank to the floor, leaning against the warped cabinet fronts.

"So much dying," George said with a deep sigh.

38

Cora jumped from her chair and eased herself down beside her old friend. She was much smaller than the tall man, and couldn't really get an arm around his shoulders, although she tried. She settled for patting his knee.

"Oh, George, has Ruby died?" she asked. "Where have you been all these years?"

George wiped the back of a gnarled hand across his eyes. Then he grinned. "No, our dear little Ruby is fine. Not so little now. That's one feisty woman. She'd hardly be our baby tag-a-long. She's running the whole she-bang at a big nursing home."

The children hadn't quite known how to react to the sight of a grown man trying not to cry, but Lindsey related to Ruby's story. She said, "Ruby was the youngest? So am I. Sometimes it's annoying."

"I understand that a little better now than I did when I was nine and Ruby was seven," George said, smiling at Lindsey.

"Who died?" Sunny asked bluntly. "My mother was killed when I was very small, but we didn't know until a couple of years ago. I barely remember her. Miss Ana helped figure out who did it. She's trying to solve two mysteries right now. There's a man who sings on the river at night, and some other man got shot in town."

Jimmie was grinning from ear to ear. "Here's your singer, Ana."

I had suspected as much. I pulled George to his feet and motioned him into the chair. Cora stood behind him and rested a hand on his shoulder.

"What is the instrument you play?" I asked. "And why are your songs so sad?"

"Open that box." George pointed at the long case.

Jimmie stepped forward and released the catches. He lifted the hinged lid. Displayed on a bed of dark red velvet was an instrument that looked something like a stretched out violin, but it had steel strings and a short neck.

"It's a mountain dulcimer," George said. He stood and lifted it from the case. Placing it across his knees, he pulled a pick from his shirt pocket and began to play "Swing Low Sweet Chariot." With the fingers of his left hand he pressed on the strings, and with the pick in his right hand, he strummed. The metallic music and George's beautiful baritone voice filled the room. After George sang it once, we all joined in. After several more songs, George laid the dulcimer back in the case.

"I like that a lot," Beth said. "Maybe you could show me how to play."

Sunny, however, continued to take charge of the conversation. "When Jimmie almost caught you, Miss Ana thought you might have been my dad, come back to see where my mom's body was found. It was on Ana's property by the river."

George stared at Sunny, the whites of his eyes showing. He seemed disturbed by Sunny's information, but I couldn't imagine why.

"Who is your father?" he said. "I'm pretty sure I'm not related to you, but anything is possible."

"My dad is DuWayne Jefferson, but Star and I use Grandpa's last name, Leonard. Dad is from Chicago. Do you know him?"

"I can't say that I do, young lady. But I'm pleased to meet you. And your friends. I've been feeling sorry for myself because my wife, Selma, died. She'd been sick with cancer for so long, and I finally lost her about a month ago."

"Why did you come here?" Beth asked.

George wiped a hand across his eyes again and began with a question.

"Do you children know what it's like to lose someone you care about?"

"I just told you about my mom," Sunny said. "My older sister, Star, does remember her, and our dad doesn't pay us much attention. We're lucky to have a grandfather who takes care of us."

Lindsey spoke up. "Beth and I had to live with our dad when we were little because our mom— that's Jimmie's mom too— was being kept like a prisoner by a man she married. Ana helped Mom get away, and now we're back together. But it was bad for a long time. It was like we had lost both Mom and Jimmie."

"Our dad is OK, but he doesn't know much about girls," Beth added.

George nodded. "I think maybe you do understand. Well, after I lost my Selma, my sister, Ruby, thought we should sell this property. I said I'd come look it over. But while I was here, I got to thinking about another person I lost here, on the river."

Cora grimaced and squeezed George's shoulder. "I remember," she said.

"What happened?" I asked, searching for an answer in George's face.

"My daddy drowned on the river. His name was Martin Harris, and he was the best father a boy could ask for. He worked all his life at the canning factory that Cora's father managed. We were very poor when I was small, but Dad worked hard, and he had integrity and mechanical talent. He was promoted to foreman of the maintenance crew. After that, we were regular middle-class folks. Mr. Dubois, that's Cora's dad, took some flack for placing a black man in such a position back in those days. But he stuck by his decision and helped us all believe that other things were more important than the color of a person's skin."

"So, that's why you've been singing on the river. Because of your dad? But why near my house?"

"His boat washed up on shore on the Mosher farm. I guess that's your property now. He died after I'd grown up, but I just had to go back there and mourn for Selma and Daddy. Guess I was singing for Sunny's mother, too, whether I knew it or not. I didn't mean to cause you any grief. I didn't even know who you were when I first went there."

"It's a lonely stretch of the river," I said.

"Sing for us again," Lindsey commanded.

"Yes, do," Sunny added. "Don't be sad. We'll help you feel better."

George picked up the dulcimer again and played some chords. He sang, "Abide with me, fast falls the eventide. The darkness deepens, Lord, with me abide."

The children did not know the song, but Cora and I joined in. After a few times through we all sang the ending together. "When other helpers fail and comforts flee, help of the helpless, oh, abide with me."

Jimmie sang with enthusiasm, but his voice squeaked uncontrollably at awkward places. He blushed, but George grinned at him, laid aside the dulcimer and clapped him on the back. "You'll be a fine singer in about a year, son."

39

"Where's your car, George?" I asked. "And why have you been so secretive? Grieving a loss isn't anything to be ashamed of."

George hung his head. "You're right, of course. I guess I was just being selfish, not wanting anyone to know I was back in town. I've been gone for years. I didn't know how people would treat me."

"People are the same as always," Cora said bluntly. "Some are good, and some aren't."

"Selma grew up where there was no respect for people like us. She wasn't good at facing the difficulties of life. She believed it was better to hide your feelings than to deal with them. Some of her thinking must have rubbed off on me." George put his hands over his face.

Cora moved around in front of George and took his hands in her own. "Remember who you are. There were so many challenging situations that came our way when we were children. You were always right there with us, helping to solve the problems, not giving in to them. All right, so Selma's gone. All our parents are gone. Our friend, Jimmie, too. I lost one husband when the canning factory blew up. But we have this Jimmie. Sunny, and Beth and Lindsey are right here in front of you. Don't you have children, George? Grandchildren?"

"I do. They are precious to me. The youngest grandson is just learning to walk."

"Fight the gloom, George. Dwelling on these losses is not the same as dealing with them. Life goes on, but you still have people who love you. Ruby, me, the rest of your family." Cora leaned forward and kissed her friend on the top of his head.

The kids were losing patience with this serious conversation. "What's your grandson's name?" Jimmy asked.

"Yeah," Beth chimed in. "Do they live around here? How old are the rest? Can we play with them? We are always looking for other kids to play ball."

"Are any of them our age?" Sunny asked. "Maybe we know them from school."

George reached out and took Cora's hands in his. He smiled. "I've been an old fool. It's all right to grieve, but now I think it's time to stop hiding on the river."

Lindsey jumped up, ran to George and hugged him. "We'll be your friends."

"And I'll tell you about my grandchildren."

"Let's sing some more," Beth urged.

Just then Cora's phone rang. "Oh my, it's almost four o'clock," Cora said after she pulled it from her pocket and looked at the screen. "Hello, dear."

There was a pause. The kids were now crowding around George, asking more questions, but whispering so as not to disturb Cora's phone call.

"I had no idea it was getting so late. It will take me an hour to get home. You'd better make our apologies. You'll never guess who I'm bringing home for dinner... Yes, I'm sure it's more important than one of your advertisers. It's George Harris!"

George was reaching once more for the dulcimer, but Cora changed his plans.

"George, you need to pack up your things and get ready to come stay in town for now. You've had your time alone on the river with your thoughts, but now you're going to have a hot meal and sleep in a bed. I suppose you've been curled up on the bare floor with some old blankets..."

I thought she was being dramatic, but George's sheepish look confirmed her accusation.

"But my car..." George protested.

"What car?"

"It's over in the lane that leads down to River Road. That way I could just walk from the back of the house and no one would see it or even see a path leading to the road from the house."

Cora had clearly taken charge. "Leave it for tonight. We'll deal with what you need tomorrow."

"I'm not poor, Cora. Just temporarily in a bad place."

But Cora was having none of it. "You're coming with me. I have to hear about your kids, and Ruby. Maybe even your crazy cousins. Go collect your things."

"Yes, ma'am," George said, rolling his eyes at the rest of us in mock exasperation. But he meekly started up the stairs. As he did so, he called over his shoulder, "You're my senior by five months, so I guess you've got the right to boss me around." Then he grinned.

As we soon realized, we couldn't fit another adult in my Jeep and even remotely pretend to be legal, so George needed to drive his own car to town after all.

Cora apparently thought she would have to stay with George to be sure he didn't simply drive away.

He shook his head meekly and allowed her to plan the rest of his day.

I thought we'd had enough surprises for one afternoon, but there was one more yet in store.

"You wait for us at the bottom of the hill," Cora instructed me. "I want to go down toward the confluence."

Not having a clue what she was thinking, but certain she knew there was no longer a bridge where the Thorpe met the Petite Sauble, I simply agreed.

While the kids and I waited at the corner, the girls rummaged in the back, and all were soon munching their way through the rest of the potato chips and cookies.

"We should have grabbed some bottles of water," Jimmie said.

"But that water belongs to George," Sunny said.

"Check the lemonade jug. Maybe there's some left."

Just then, a gray hatchback with a canoe rack on top appeared to our right. I could see Cora in the passenger seat pointing past the intersection. I pulled out behind her. Our short caravan proceeded to the somewhat dilapidated white house that was the only building on this stretch of road. I knew it all too well. It was where I'd discovered who had been responsible for Sunny's mother's death.

The hatchback pulled into the overgrown driveway, and the doors opened. I parked behind it and we all rolled out.

Cora stood resting one hand on the hood of George's car, and she was studying the old, square two-story house.

Now George put his hand on Cora's shoulder. He leaned over and whispered something to her. She reached back and laid her hand over his.

"Memories," she said. "You can let them eat you, or you can get on with your life."

This seemed like such a strange thing for the self-proclaimed county historian to say that I asked, "What do you mean? Why did you bring us here?"

Cora shook her head as if to clear it. "Oh, well. We were already on this side of the river, so it seemed fitting to take the extra minute to come here. Haven't I ever told you? This is the house where I grew up."

40

"I told you to just sit tight. Keep a low profile. They can't prove a thing."

41

I fell asleep that night thinking warm sentimental thoughts of "my" singer, George, feeling happy that Cora had been reunited with her childhood friend.

***

The lack of solutions for my other mystery hit me hard the next morning as Jerry Caulfield called me before I had finished my requisite three cups of coffee.

"There was a fax in the tray for you when I came in this morning," he said. "From California. You requested a copy of Rudolf Schoellkopf's will? That's Chester's father?"

"It is, and I did. Just checking to make sure Adele's hero is as rich as she claims."

"Looks pretty real, unless he's lost it all somehow. Stop by and pick up the paperwork on your next trip to town."

"Will do."

I had taken two more sips of coffee, and the phone rang again. This time it was Adele.

"You'll never believe who was in the store this morning!"

It sounded as if Adele had calmed down enough to be back to her gossipy self.

She forged ahead without waiting for a response from me. "George Harris! He's been gone since I was a teenager. His wife has died and he's back in the area to look at the family home..."

I hadn't said a word yet, and Adele stopped in the middle of her run-on sentence.

"You aren't asking me who he is. You already know him?"

Glad she couldn't see me smirk, I understated the depth of my knowledge to let her continue in her joy of discovery, "Yes, I met him yesterday."

"Well, stop by later, and I'll tell you all about it."

I promised.

An hour and an extra cup of coffee later, I entered the Cherry Hill police station. It was only Thursday, but that Tuesday-deadline clock for my crime column was already ticking in my head. I needed updates. Tracy was behind her desk, and I asked her if there was anything new on the murder case. After all, it had been twenty-four hours since I'd checked in. The whole thing might be solved by now.

Not a chance of that, Tracy assured me. But she did have some news on the bullets.

"We got a report back that the bullets from the derringer only had smudges. The one in the wall hit brick and was pretty flat anyway. There was one partial fingerprint on one of the casings. Can't connect it to anyone."

"Derringers have only two shots, right?" I asked. I know next to nothing about handguns, but this information had stuck somewhere in my brain.

"Right. The term has come to mean pretty much any very small handgun that is neither a revolver nor an automatic. There's no room for any moving parts. They have two barrels, two bullets, two shots."

"Awfully small for someone with large hands."

"Agreed. That lends some credence to Chet's claim that he bought it for his wife. Women tend to like the size. The downside is that most derringers only shoot small caliber rounds. This one usually takes a twenty-two long, although it will also fire a twenty-two rimfire Magnum. That has a little more punch, and it's what our two bullets are."

"Does that mean anything special," I asked.

"Maybe. Maybe not. It's certainly a good choice if you want to have a better chance of killing someone because they have a higher velocity. Standard twenty-twos can be lethal, but you need a really accurate shot into a vital area. Still in all, they are small bullets. Small weapon– small projectiles. It's just the way it is."

I was scribbling in a small notebook as fast as possible. "Even if you can't make a good match with the partial print, does it rule anyone out?"

Tracy wasn't one to telegraph her feelings when she was uncomfortable, but it sure looked to me as if she squirmed.

"It doesn't match any of Lyle's prints. We can't rule it out for one of Chet's fingers. We have two matching points of identification. As you know, we need a lot more than that– twelve points for a legal match. And the partial on this casing could be from any portion of any finger of the person who loaded the gun, rotated in any direction. It's not like partials come with register marks for lining things up."

"And this was on the fatal bullet?"

"The casing of the first bullet fired. The one that killed Lyle."

"How do you know which one was first?"

"The hammer was in the lower position when the gun was turned over to us, so we know the top bullet was fired first."

"So a crafty prosecutor could say that one of Chester's fingerprints was found on the bullet that killed Lyle," I said.

"The casing," Tracy corrected. "He or she could, but probably wouldn't." She shifted in her seat again. "Look, I don't want to weaken our possible case, but a good defense attorney would turn right around and point out that you could probably get two matching points with at least half the population. He would ask which of Chet's fingers was a match, and the prosecutor would have to say 'his fifth.'"

I looked up in surprise. "Not too many people would use their pinky finger to load a bullet into a gun of any kind."

"Exactly. And if the defense attorney were into showmanship, he'd bring in a projector and demonstrate that he could get two points of identification on this partial in evidence to match his own prints. Or the judge's wife's. A prosecutor that didn't see that coming wouldn't be worth re-electing. This really doesn't mean much."

"But it does seem to rule out that Lyle loaded the gun, and maybe Chester did bring it with him."

"That's is certainly what it suggests," Tracy admitted. "However..."

"There's a however?"

"There is. We were able to trace where this batch of bullets was distributed for sale. They all went to stores in southern California six years ago, including a gun shop in Marina Del Ray."

"Marina Del Ray, California. Where Lyle has been living."

"Yes."

"And Chester claims he hasn't even seen Lyle in five years," I said.

"That's what he says."

"Have you checked the partial with Tucker's prints? How about Chester's wife or Lyle's? Can you get any of their prints?"

"Tucker's in the clear."

I thought about that for a minute. "He is for the actual shooting, but the gun could have been loaded any time. What if he's in cahoots with someone? You know I've wondered about that off and on since the beginning."

"True enough. I can see if any of those people have prints on file."

Then I had a brain wave. "You know what family member does have a record? Eva. That's who. She's in the system for various drug charges."

"I'll check it out," Tracy said, "Although I need to remind you again that two points of identification mean nothing for a positive ID."

42

I knew that Tracy had officially interviewed Charlie, owner of the pharmacy and the apartment where Lyle was killed. But I figured it wouldn't hurt for me to talk to him as well. He might give me some details that would flesh out a good news column.

The walk along Main Street was a good reminder of how close Volger's Grocery was to the drugstore. It probably hadn't taken Chester more than a few minutes to walk the distance. With the uncertainty surrounding the exact time of the lethal shot, his register receipt wasn't much of an alibi.

Charlie was swiping at the window display with the modern equivalent of a feather duster– a handle with strips of soft papery cloth attached. His bald head shone with perspiration.

"It's supposed to electrostatically attract the dust, but I think it just stirs things up," Charlie said, pointing to a ribbon of sunlight filled with tiny floating motes. "What can I do for you today, Ana?"

"Hi Charlie! I'm wondering if you'd mind telling me what happened the morning Lyle was shot. Maybe give me some interesting detail I can use in the paper?"

He stepped down from the small ladder he'd been standing on. "Sure. Come on back."

I followed him down the narrow aisle lined with lotions, beach toys, anti-itch cream, ace bandages, and much more. The shelves were full. Charlie's business was apparently doing well. We reached the pharmacy counter, and he swiveled the computer monitor to face both of us.

"Here's what I showed Tracy." His fingers danced over the keyboard and various windows popped onto the screen. "The dispensary software logs every time the file is saved. I was filling prescriptions that morning– see the date here." He pointed to a line in one of the window bars. "So, I saved the file at ten-thirty, ten-forty-three, and ten-fifty-six. I'm not absolutely certain, but I think I heard what turned out to be the gunshot between those first two times."

"You aren't positive?"

"Like I told Tracy… it was just some noise. I didn't know there'd been a murder or that everything was going to depend on what time it occurred. How often do you check the time when you hear a slightly unusual noise?"

"OK, I get it. But why didn't you check on the noise right then?" I asked.

"I thought it was some old car in the alley, backfiring. It wasn't all that loud. And I was counting out some capsules. I just kept doing that. But when the bottle was filled, and I logged that in," he pointed to the 10:42 time stamp, "I started thinking about it."

"And you went upstairs?"

"Not yet. It hadn't yet entered my mind that I'd heard a gunshot. I just started filling the next scrip."

"Then what?"

"I was counting the lisinopril for Mrs. Adamcek– that's for her high blood pressure. Don't say I told you, though. I'm not supposed to reveal information like this, although I'm sure everyone at her bridge club and half the town knows it. Anyway, I realized the pop hadn't come from the alley. It had been more like over my head. Made no sense at all. So, I finished and saved that file…"

"The ten-fifty-six time."

Charlie nodded. "I logged out– can't leave the computer unattended and open for fiddling– and went outside and up the stairs. There's no entrance from inside the store. By this time I was concerned, otherwise I wouldn't have gone out since I was the only employee in the store."

"You didn't hear anyone on the stairs?"

"Nope, I never do. The exterior brick wall is between the store and the stairwell, not to mention the insulation, wallboard, shelving and stocked goods on this side of the bricks."

I'd heard the rest of the story several times from both Tracy and Chester, but I wanted to hear it from Charlie. "Go on."

"I got to the top of the stairs, and the apartment door was wide open. The blond guy that rented the apartment was standing there with his back to me, and a chubby fellow was on the floor. There was a spilled sack of groceries beside him. I said, 'What's going on here?' and the guy who was standing swung around and shot a little pistol. I don't know if he meant to shoot at me, but it sure felt like it. Hit the wall, though."

"That's Chester Schoellkopf."

"He's the one. But he didn't try to run away. He looked down at the gun in his hand as if it were some kind of surprise to find it there, and then he dropped it. He just stood there looking at me."

"Did he say anything?"

"Nope. Just froze, like he was in shock."

I thought for a minute. "Who called the police?"

"I did."

"But Chester didn't try to run away or stop you from making the call?"

"Not in any way. He seemed almost relieved."

This was interesting. I hadn't heard a thing before now about how Chester had acted during this time. His lack of emotion was quite different from the blustering and angry demeanor I'd usually seen. Did this indicate that he was in shock and had nothing to do with the crime, or was it a sign that he was a cold-blooded killer?

I had one more question. "If someone other than Chester shot Lyle, that person could have come down the stairs, and you wouldn't have seen them?"

"Sure. Especially if they turned left and didn't pass in front of the store. But there's another option too."

"What's that?"

"There's a fire escape out the kitchen window. Seems a little silly for such a small apartment, but to rent it out, I have to have two exits to meet regulations."

This was also new information. I hadn't thought about a fire escape. "Can I see it?" I asked.

"The apartment's still sealed, but just walk around behind the building in the alley and you'll find it."

"Thanks, Charlie," I said, "This has been a great help."

Charlie gave me a two-finger salute. "Same thing I told Kyle and Tracy, but you're welcome."

I exited, and walked down the block to the alley which led to the backs of the Main Street stores. I thought I might have trouble picking out the correct building from the back side, but it turned out to be easy. There was only one fire escape leading from any second floor of the buildings between me and Cherry Street. It consisted of a vertical ladder affixed to the brick which climbed just high enough so that cars and small trucks could pass under the platform which extended from a window.

This was not like a city fire escape which would be inaccessible from street level. Anyone could have entered that way as well as exited. The alley was deserted, and it was now approximately the same time of day as when the shooting had occurred. I needed to check with the occupants of the other buildings that backed up to this alley.

43

The local police had probably already interviewed everyone who might have seen anything, but I was still hoping for some human interest angle that I could use for my crime column. I went back to the middle of this half block and looked more closely at the buildings that flanked the alley.

Right beside the fire escape was an extremely narrow dead-end opening between the drugstore and the building beside it. I realized this had to be the alley side of the space occupied by the stairs to the apartment. Several trash cans were stuffed in it and beyond them an old, rusting, one-speed bicycle was propped against the brick wall. Unbelievably, I could not remember what was in the building next to the drugstore, but the two windows and the pane in the door that flanked on the alley were painted black. Not likely anyone had seen something through those.

Beyond the fire escape was the rear door of the drugstore. I knew this was a public entrance with a narrow hallway flanking the office and actual pharmacy. Anyone using that would have been seen by Charlie. And beyond that was Cherry Street.

The remainder of this portion of the block was filled by the bank building. Compared to modern banks, this was tiny. It had been the State Bank forever, but just a few years ago had sold out to Wells Fargo. They still provided basic services, but there wasn't even room for a drive-up window. The alley side of the brick building was broken only by one steel door. There were no windows.

I turned around to check the buildings that faced Taylor, the next street north. At the intersection of the two alleys in the middle of the block was a small municipal parking lot with a dumpster. Just west of that were two more parking spaces and the recessed back door of a one-story business. A small hand-lettered sign read, "Tara's Hair Care. Walk-Ins Welcome. Use Front Door. Private Parking." This business also had no back windows.

The rest of this block's quadrant was occupied by a vintage private residence. The well-kept lawn was surrounded by a hedge, except for a driveway that led off the alley to a single-car garage. The house faced Cherry Street. There were lots of windows on the alley side, and lawn furniture in the open area. Maybe the occupants of that house had seen something.

Time to get busy. First, I walked around to Main Street to see what was in the building beside the drugstore. No wonder I couldn't remember. It was empty. There was a faded sign for Thousand Lakes Real Estate in the window. Understandably, this storefront wasn't in high demand; the building was barely twenty-five feet wide. I shook my head in bewilderment at the business expectations of early twentieth-century architects.

I stepped into the bank. Lyle had been shot on Saturday, and the bank was open Saturday mornings, so at least this building hadn't also been empty at the time of the murder. I went straight to the office of Gilbert Messler, Vice President. He'd approved the loans for my house renovations, and I'd never been late on a payment. He was sure to offer whatever assistance he could.

Mr. Messler was polite and almost eager to help, but he assured me he'd interviewed every employee, and no one had heard a thing. The bank walls were thick.

I walked all the way around the block to the front door of Tara's Hair Care on Taylor Street. I did not know Tara. Fleetingly, I wondered why, and when I stepped inside I saw Peggy Cowell brandishing a comb and leaning over an elderly woman.

"Hi Peggy," I said.

"Hi, Ana," she greeted me in return.

"I didn't know you work for someone named Tara. Isn't this your place?"

Peggy laughed and swiveled the woman around so she could see herself in the mirror.

The woman smiled and touched her newly dyed curls.

"I bought the business and the name," Peggy said. "Tara moved on years ago. Her ex wouldn't leave her alone. Do you want a trim? I've got a free time slot. Just give me another few minutes with Mrs. Dawson."

While Peggy finished up with the older woman, I looked in the mirror myself. Well, I did look a bit ragged around the edges. My long-ish pageboy was getting decidedly too long I was soon going to need to ponytail it. The dishwater blond color of my hair wasn't attractive, but I didn't care very much.

"Well?"

"OK, Give me something shorter for summer."

"How about some highlights?" Peggy suggested.

"Well, why not?" I decided.

By the time I left Tara's Hair Care, I knew that the house next door was owned by Otto and Julianne Osmo, a middle-aged couple who attended the Lutheran Church. Peggy thought they didn't go out much in the summer, and they spent winters with their son and his family in Arizona.

I heard a long list of complaints about how unauthorized people parked in her two private spaces all the time, apparently not wanting to walk the extra twenty feet from the public lot to the drugstore. That prompted me to ask if she'd seen anyone do that the past Saturday. That possibility was too good to be true. She'd been so busy she hadn't stepped outside the shop all day.

It was after noon when I emerged feeling lighter and happier. The attractive cut should last the rest of the summer, and would be easy to care for.

I'd promised to see Adele, and I was hungry. I walked back around to the front of the drugstore, set the stopwatch on my cell phone, and headed for Volger's Grocery.

44

Two minutes and twenty-two seconds later, I pushed open the front door of Adele's store and was momentarily shocked into inaction. The store was packed. Then I realized the store was packed with little girls.

Adele saw me enter and her jaw dropped. "Your hair! I love it."

"Peggy's work. What's all this?" I waved a hand to take in the busy aisles.

Adele grinned. "Girl Scouts. There's a campout this weekend and they have to do their own shopping. Give me a minute."

The first wave hit the checkout counter, and Adele respectfully rang up the two or three items from each girl, carefully counting out the change from the crumpled dollar bills they handed her. One had a can of vegetable soup, and a box of foil. The next had an onion and two potatoes. Then came a box of graham crackers clutched tightly by the smallest of the girls. Of course, marshmallows and chocolate bars followed. The single leader queued up at the end of the line. She finally reached the register and paid for two pounds of ground beef. She thanked Adele for her patience. "This is why we shop at your store. You don't get impatient with this process." She looked toward the door and called, "Lizzie, please don't grab Alicia's items. I'll be right there." She rolled her eyes.

"I'm happy to help the Scouts understand how a couple of dollars from each of them can feed the whole group," Adele said. She was beaming. I thought of her late husband, Henry, and how, so many years ago, she had chosen the small-town-grocery life over high society with Chester.

Through the front door, I heard a scream and a child's voice boomed, "Lizzie, don't!"

"Gotta go. Now," the Scout leader said, and she bolted.

Finally, the store was clear. "That's more excitement than I usually see on a Thursday," Adele said.

I had gotten in line behind the Scout leader with a tub of macaroni salad and a cold drink. I pulled out my wallet and asked, "Can I borrow a fork?"

"Sure thing. Come in the office."

Adele and I moved to the enclosed space at the front of the store with its full picture window..

She pulled a fork from a mug full of utensils, handed it to me, and plunged right into the biggest news. "Do you know who George Harris is? It's so unexpected that he's come back!"

I peeled the lid of the clear plastic salad tub and scooped up a good-sized mouthful. "Tell me," I prompted.

"Well, he and Cora and our Jimmie's grandfather were the best of friends. They were in the same class at the Cherry Pit Junction Elementary. George's little sister, Ruby, and another boy— I can't remember his name— hung out together. They are older than me, of course, but we all heard about them. They developed quite a reputation for figuring out puzzles. They found things for people, and liked to help those who needed a hand. They even solved a couple of crimes."

I couldn't keep up the deception without risking Adele's feelings being hurt. "I think the other boy's name is Laszlo."

Adele put her hands on her hips and glared at me. "How do you know all this?"

Laughing, I quickly swallowed a lump of salad to prevent choking on it and said, "George Harris is my mysterious singer. I told you I met him yesterday."

"Of all the..."

"Oh, don't get uptight, Adele. You couldn't have known unless he told you. "He's a wonderful baritone, and that instrument he's been playing is a mountain dulcimer. I think we could get him to sing at church."

Adele launched into telling me more stories that had survived about the legendary friends of Cherry Pit Junction while I finished my salad. I decided I'd better get Cora to verify some of these fantastic tales. Maybe we'd write some of them down.

Finally, I wiped my hands on a paper napkin and took out my notebook and pencil. "Let's see if we can do something constructive to help Chester. I want to compare some of these times."

I wrote down:

10:30 Charlie saves a file on his computer
Charlie hears a pop- in this time slot, he thinks
10:41 grocery receipt time stamp
10:43 Charlie saves file
Charlie is sure he filled Mrs. Adamcek's prescription here
10:56 Charlie saves file
Charlie goes upstairs, startles Chester, who shoots gun
11:08 Charlie calls police

When I showed it to Adele, I said, "Can you see anything wrong with this?"

"Not really. It looks to me as if Chet should be one-hundred percent in the clear because of that receipt."

"It appears that way, but here's the problem. I did a little research. The times on Charlie's computer are probably accurate. His computer is tied to an industry-based internet clock. That's also why our cell phones all agree on the time. The police station is tied to the same program. What I'm not sure about is your cash register. It's not a computerized system, is it?"

"I don't know," Adele said, suddenly getting a slightly worried look. "Why wouldn't it be?"

"I mean, does the time the machine prints on the register tape set itself automatically, or do you have to fix it yourself? Like when the power goes out."

An emotion approaching horror was spreading across Adele's features. She answered slowly. "It's an old system. I got it secondhand– refurbished. I... I don't need state of the art technology for my little store. I do have to reset it myself."

"OK, don't panic," I said. "A small time difference won't mean much but it will be good to be sure of the facts. You go to the register and wait for me to signal you. I'll call Charlie, and then you generate a 'no sale' receipt."

"Oh, Ana, can't you just compare it to your phone time if they are all the same? I don't want to put Chester in more jeopardy."

"We could, but this will be absolutely certain proof. You know we can't hide this information no matter how it turns out."

I called the drugstore, and explained what we were doing. When I said, "now." Adele punched the register, and Charlie called out the time.

It was 1:13 Charlie time, and 1:10 Adele time. So Chester had actually checked out three minutes earlier than the time on his receipt, at 10:38 by Charlie/computer time. It took about 2.5 minutes for him to walk to the apartment. This new information did not help Chester at all. It would have been tight, but he could possibly have made it home and shot Lyle before 10:43 when Charlie next saved his file.

After I explained it to her, Adele wailed, "What have we done? This isn't helping Chet at all."

45

We talked a few more minutes. I asked Adele if Chet had left the store immediately after paying for his groceries or if they had visited a bit longer. She wanted to say he'd lingered, but admitted that even if she had wanted to fudge the time, Janice Preston had been right behind Chet. She would remember that he'd exited the store promptly.

I stopped at the newspaper office and retrieved the faxed copy of Rudolf Schoellkopf's will. It took only a few minutes to verify what Jerry had said on the phone. The vast majority of the Schoellkopf estate had been left directly to Chester with no restrictions on the use of the money. So unless some financial disaster had occurred, one that I hadn't yet discovered, Chester was more than well off. Maybe he was a gambler? As I drove south out of town, I pondered how I could find the answer to that question.

The small sign for Thousand Lakes Realty zipped by my window as I picked up speed outside the village limits. I jammed on the brakes and did a U-turn. It was a long shot, but I had nothing to lose by talking to someone about the empty storefront next to the drugstore.

The small concrete-block building that housed the real estate office had been dressed up with a fake shingled gable roof on the front. A man wearing a blue shirt with no tie looked up from a computer screen as I entered.

"Anastasia Raven! What brings you here? Hoping to buy a little more riverfront?"

I was only mildly surprised at the greeting. Now that I was a regular writer for the *Cherry Hill Herald*, most people recognized me.

The man stood and held out a hand. "Pat Morgan, at your service."

We shook, and he motioned me toward a comfortable seat as he swiveled his office chair to face me and settled himself.

"I'm really just looking for some information about an empty building in town," I began.

"Oh? Planning to open a new business?"

That idea made me pause. There was no way I wanted to be tied up in town all the time. "No. I'm not in the market for anything. I just have a few questions about the narrow building next to the drugstore."

"That listing is a real problem. It's a prime location, but it's so small that most potential buyers won't even look at it. Not that we have a long list of prospects for commercial enterprises in Cherry Hill." He sounded rueful.

"Sure. I can understand that. I'm really wondering if you know of anyone who might have been using the building last Saturday. You know, when the shooting took place in the apartment over the drugstore. I'm trying to find anyone who might have seen or heard something."

Pat looked thoughtful. "It's funny you should ask about Saturday. Remind me what time it all happened."

"The time can't be nailed down exactly. Probably not before ten-thirty in the morning, and certainly no later than ten-forty-three by computer or cell-phone time."

"Hmm. That's not when I was in town. I was there earlier."

"But you saw something unusual? Why is it odd that I'm asking?"

The realtor stood and walked to a coffee machine that rested on a counter along the side wall. "Want some?" he asked.

"Sure. Black," I said.

He returned to his chair, and handed me a foam cup of coffee. Surprisingly, it wasn't burned. He continued. "This must have been around ten, but I'll admit I wasn't paying strict attention to the time. And it has nothing to do with that empty building. It's probably meaningless"

"Try me," I urged.

"Well, I went to town that morning, even though it was Saturday, because we picked up a new listing on Meadow Street. It's near the corner of Peach. I wanted to get the For Sale signs up right away. It's an attractive small house; someone might want to grab it for a summer home."

I tried to picture this location and realized it was a block south and west of the drugstore.

Pat continued. "There was a car parked in front of the house."

"That was unusual? I don't understand."

"Of course not. It's a street with public parking. But a two-thousand five Acura was there." He grinned like a ten-year-old. "'Blast Orange' color– limited edition. Not too many of those around, and I was surprised because I used to have a car just like that, and I hated it because of that color. Momentarily, I wondered if it was my old car, so I looked for a scrape on the front quarter panel that I'd gotten in a parking lot. But it wasn't the same vehicle."

Frankly, I was disappointed. This didn't sound like it was remotely related to the shooting. I said as much.

Pat waved a hand. "As I said, probably nothing. But you asked for anything out of the ordinary, and I've never seen a car like that around town before."

"Did you happen to notice the license plate?"

"Nope. Except that it was muddy. The whole car was. It had definitely been on some dirt roads."

"And you didn't see anyone drive it away?"

I stuck my signs in the lawn, checked to make sure the house was locked and left. It could still be there for all I know."

I thanked Pat Morgan for his time and the coffee. Instead of going home, I drove back to Cherry Hill. It was highly unlikely the car would still be there. Certainly one of the neighbors would have complained about a muddy, abandoned car on their street. Tracy or Kyle would have noticed it on their regular rounds if it were still there. They probably knew every vehicle in the village by sight. Nevertheless, I turned west on Meadow when I got back into town. I easily located the house with the Thousand Lakes Realty sign in the lawn, but there was no orange car at the curb.

This train of thought led me to another difficulty. Neglecting the question of why Lyle had tracked down his father, how had Lyle gotten to Chester's apartment on that fateful Saturday?

46

I drove to the police station. Tracy was at her desk doing paperwork. Kyle Appledorn, the other regular officer who was usually on patrol was also there, swigging a cup of coffee and chatting with Bob the office man.

"What did you do to your hair?" Tracy asked.

I shrugged. "It will be nice for summer," I said.

You here to see Chet again?"

Rolling my eyes, I answered, "Not unless he insists. But I have a couple of questions first, and I may have a tiny bit of helpful information."

"You share first. I could use a break in this case."

"Fair enough," I said, sitting in the empty chair across from Tracy's desk. Kyle came over to join us, and I continued. "Pat Morgan, the realtor, saw a car he didn't recognize about two blocks from the drugstore just before the shooting took place."

Kyle chuckled, "He thinks he knows every car in Cherry Hill?"

I shrugged. "Maybe he does. Anyway, he noticed this one for two reasons. It was muddy, and it was just like one he used to own. He was pretty sure there's not another in the area."

"License number?"

"Nope."

Tracy sighed. "That was probably too much to expect."

I gave her the information I had, and told her the car was not there now. "Of course not– that would be too easy." She called across the room, "Bob, did you get that?"

"Sure did," Bob called back. His fingers were tapping the keyboard. "We'll see if any of our people of interest have a connection to a vehicle of that description."

"Well, it's better than a poke in the eye. All right, what do you want from me?" Tracy asked.

"I'd like to know how Lyle got to his father's apartment, or even how he got to this area. You never told me anything about those issues."

Grinning, Tracy said, "I wondered when you'd get around to this."

"You have info you haven't told me?"

"We aren't required to tell you everything, even if you are 'the press.'" She was still grinning.

"Spill it!"

Tracy deflated. "It's not very exciting, and we didn't learn a single helpful thing. He had a key in his pocket for the Sleep Lodge in Emily City. His car– not an Acura– was still parked in their lot. In his room we found only what was expected. Sales binders from his company, lists of prospective customers, clothes. Looked like he was on an ordinary business trip. He did have one of those pre-paid burner phones with a couple of calls on it, but they led us nowhere. Both were to another burner. The one real anomaly is that the car keys were in the ignition, and the car wasn't locked. And, I suppose it's a little odd that it hadn't been stolen. That would have complicated this mess even more."

"So, how did he get to Cherry Hill?"

"We don't know."

"And you don't think it's suspicious that the keys were in his car?"

Kyle couldn't take it any longer. "Of course we do, Ana. We checked the car for fingerprints but any that weren't smudges belonged to Lyle."

Before I could stop myself, I blurted out, "And you checked the back of the rearview mirror?"

Bristling, Kyle erupted. "You think we're hick cops, too? I've had about enough of you people from big cities."

I regretted my comment instantly. "I'm sorry. Probably too much TV." The truth was that I rarely watched television, but I had to blame something for my boorishness.

Tracy stepped in. "We're all on edge. This case seems to go nowhere, and our resources keep getting diverted with these petty thefts. There was another break-in last night on the east end of Taylor Street."

Across the room, Bob sucked in a breath. The sharp sound cut the tension, and we all turned his way.

"Blast Orange Acura, 2005, owner of record is Eva Ashlynn Schoellkopf. Residence listed as 523 Arroyo Drive, El Centro, California," he read from the screen.

"Perhaps there are more fingers in this pie than we realized," Tracy said, her eyes sparking. "Kyle, go get Chester."

"Yes, ma'am!"

A couple of minutes later, Chester was seated near Tracy's desk. He was handcuffed, and I noticed a short chain connected his ankles.

"Tell us again. When was the last time you saw your granddaughter," Tracy asked.

Chester began twisting his head, looking me over. "You did something to your hair. What does it matter when I saw Eva?'"

When no one responded, Chester began to study our faces.

A crafty smile spread slowly across his face. "She's turned up here, hasn't she? That girl is just too smart for her own good. Smart like a cobra. But maybe she's met her mongoose."

Tracy cleared her throat. "We don't know if she's here or not, but there is evidence that suggests she has been in the area. Again, when did you last see Eva?"

Chester was more sure of himself now. He leaned back in the chair and laced his fingers behind his head. The handcuffs clinked. "I'd have to figure it out. Maybe around five or six years ago. I think she was sixteen. Yeah, sixteen. Kicking up a fuss at being told what to do, she never showed up for her own sixteenth birthday party."

"You didn't see her last week?"

"Last week? Not on your life. I did see her once after that party, though. She was mad as a hornet. Didn't want Lyle running her life she told me. That was right before she ran away with the biker gang."

"How about a vehicle?" Kyle asked. "Do you know if she owned one?"

"At sixteen? No car. She couldn't even drive yet. Legally, anyway."

Tracy hammered at the timeline. "You have had no contact with Eva since she was sixteen years old? No phone conversations? Emails? Nothing?"

Chester looked smug. "Aren't you going to ask me about Morse code or smoke signals? I assure you I haven't spoken with her. But if she's here, let her deal with the funeral arrangements for her father. Maybe she knows where her mother is."

I hadn't seen a family quite so dysfunctionally hostile for a while. Certainly Eva would not have the connections to return her father's body to the family plot if she'd been out of touch for so long. Apparently, Chester realized this as well.

"The lawyer's got the funeral under control anyway. I doubt Eva can be trusted. Where did you say she is?"

"We didn't," Tracy stated flatly.

47

Chester switched gears. "Hey, this morning I thought of someone else who might have it in for my son. Have you looked at his ex-wife's family? Maybe some relative of Danielle was out to get Lyle for the way he treated her."

Kyle actually rolled his eyes. "Does that make any sense?"

Chester smirked. "It makes as much sense as me wanting to kill him, or even Eva. She got her freedom by running off and declaring herself emancipated, and now she's twenty-one. What possible benefit is there to knocking off her father at this point? And why do it thousands of miles from home? As far as I know she stayed in California, or maybe Mexico."

Personally, I thought those were pretty good questions. I almost asked a few of my own but realized that Tracy didn't want Chester to hear some of our new information.

"Take him back," Tracy said.

Kyle hauled Chester to his feet and pointed him in the direction of his cell. The suspect shuffled obediently ahead of Kyle. But when they paused as the gate to the cell block opened, Chester turned and looked at me. He was grinning from ear to ear, clearly a victory face.

After Chester was out of earshot, I told Tracy I had even more information. I explained to her about my comparison of the times between the grocery store and the pharmacy. She thanked me for this info, even if it wasn't good news for Chester and said they would also conduct an official test.

I asked if she'd followed up on the possibility that Eva had lived at a Santa Barbara commune. Of course, now that her vehicle registration showed an address that Bob said was 300 miles from Santa Barbara, this question sounded somewhat hollow.

"We did manage to talk to someone at the Clan of the Strawberry Moon."

My eyebrows lifted.

Tracy shook her head. "I don't name 'em. But, yes, she lived there for several years. Nobody asks for identification or proof of age. And they don't keep records. 'Giver of Grace' thought she might have 'moved to a new level of fulfillment' some time last year."

"Maybe because she knew her twenty-first birthday was coming up."

"Maybe, but you can do anything in California at eighteen except buy liquor or tobacco."

"Well, those might be two important reasons for her to live with a group of mixed-age people. What about that partial print? Anything there?"

Bob had returned to his computer station. He glanced at Tracy and she nodded. He said, "We've got a ten card for Eva. Ana was right. She had some drug charges as a juvie, and nothing is sealed. She kept jumping probation. We did get a match with that partial for three of her fingers."

"But remember, Ana, I warned you that means next to nothing," Tracy repeated.

I thanked them for their help, used the rest room, and headed once more for my car.

It was late afternoon by now, but not really suppertime, so I decided to visit the Osmos. I'd written down their first names, and flipped through my notebook. Otto and Julianne. Their house was the only other property on the alley behind the drugstore.

I parked on Cherry Street, and only a few seconds after I knocked on the front door, it was opened by a woman who was perhaps a few years older than I am with a smiling, open face and straight brown hair pulled back with a scrunchie. She wore jeans with dirt-smudged knees and a pink t-shirt advertising a five-kilometer race fundraiser. She followed my gaze and placed a hand over her heart. "Oh, not me. My daughter runs in so many races she gives me her extra shirts. Call me Juli," she said.

"I'm Ana. It rhymes with 'Donna.'"

"I've been working in the garden and was just about to have some iced tea. Will you join me? Otto is still at the office."

In a few minutes we were seated at a white iron filagree table surrounded by flowerbeds. From this location there was a clear view of the entire back side of the drugstore and apartment above it. The Osmos would have needed to erect a very tall fence to block the view. They had settled for a low privet hedge. The alley and the backs of the Main Street buildings weren't urban-ugly, but the worn and discolored bricks clashed with the lovely gardens in which we rested.

I explained my mission, expecting to be told that they'd been in Emily City, or away for the weekend.

"I was right here all morning, digging in the azaleas." Juli said. "A number of cars drove through the alley, but nothing out of the ordinary. A lot of people come to town on Saturday, and beyond the salon is a good place to park. It was a good move when the village knocked down the old Tuttle building and paved the space."

"Did you see anyone using the fire escape from the drugstore apartment?"

Her laugh was infectious. "Wouldn't that be something? To see a person actually climbing that awkward ladder."

I agreed that would be out of the ordinary. It was interesting that she assumed the person would be climbing rather than descending.

"I think I would have noticed, but I suppose I wasn't watching every minute," she admitted.

"What about the sound of the shot? Charlie heard it in the drugstore. If you were outside, I don't know how you could have missed it."

"Let me think," she said, resting an elbow on the table and propping her chin in her hand. Her eyes clouded over.

I sipped the tea. It was ice cold and strong. The flower gardens were gorgeous. I was beginning to like Juli Osmo.

"The compressor!"

Her outburst startled me a little and I slopped some tea on my shirt.

"Oh, dear. I'm so sorry," she said.

I grabbed one of the paper napkins she'd thoughtfully brought to the table. "Not a big deal. Tell me about the compressor."

"Well, Otto was in the garage that morning. He likes to tinker with things on Saturdays. We often go for a bicycle ride in the evenings, and he had plugged in the air compressor to fill our tires. I had one that was getting low. That thing is incredibly noisy for the few minutes it takes to get up to pressure. If we had close neighbors, I'm sure they would complain."

"And you might not have heard anything over that sound?"

"It's horrible. It's like someone is taking a jackhammer to your brain."

Now I needed to ask the critical question. "Do you have any way of knowing what time that was?"

"Of course. I was annoyed because I was on the phone with our daughter when Otto started that thing, so we had to hang up. My cell phone said it was ten-seventeen when we ended the call."

"And how long does the noise last until the compressor tank is filled?" I asked.

"I have no idea," Juli said. "I don't know how to make the infernal thing work. I'll ask Otto to time it tonight if you like. I can call you."

We exchanged phone numbers, and she urged me to join the local garden club. "If we could just get a few more members who are under seventy years old, we could make the park look really nice in the summer."

I promised to think about it and headed home.

48

Friday morning dawned gray. Juli hadn't yet called.

I decided to try to turn the scraps of fact I'd gathered into my crime column, but I just couldn't get a handle on how to start. Not only that, I hadn't verified with Tracy if it was all right to make my tidbits public. Since I'd uncovered most of the information, it was mine to use. But it doesn't pay to antagonize law enforcement in a small town.

Opening my laptop, I typed:

Mysterious Car Spotted Near Scene of Recent Murder!

I was pretty sure Tracy did not want me to make Eva's possible presence known.

Time Stamps Do Not Clear Suspect

I might be able to use that, but Adele would never forgive me. If Chester did prove to be guilty, would she place the blame on his shoulders where it belonged or fault me for uncovering evidence that helped convict him?

Partial Prints Matched to Several Suspects

OK, that would be really shabby reporting. Tracy had hammered this point over and over. The fingerprints meant next to nothing. They seemed to rule out Chester, but there was very little value in what had been found.

Neighbor Reports Alley was Empty at Time of Shooting

That wasn't even true. Juli Osmo had said there were several cars that drove through the alley. Maybe she was just distracted or bent over below the level of her hedge. She might have missed seeing someone who was agile slither down the fire escape, run to a car in the parking lot and drive away. If the person was savvy, he wouldn't have peeled out. Remaining calm would guarantee giving the impression of being an ordinary Saturday shopper.

Druggist Uncertain as to Time of Shot

Hmm. Now here was something interesting to think about. Charlie had told everyone that he wasn't positive he'd heard the popping sound between 10:30 and 10:43, but we'd all just gone with that time frame because there wasn't any reason to question it. His was the only story that provided any solid clues about the time. But what if he were mistaken? The shot couldn't have been later, but might it have been earlier?

I hunted up the phone number for the Medical Examiner that served Forest County. The office was actually in Emily City, which is in Sturgeon County. Our population is so low we don't merit one of our own. I dialed.

"Office of the Medical Examiner. How may I direct your call?" A crisp voice answered.

"This is Anastasia Raven, calling from the *Cherry Hill Herald*. I'd like to speak to the Medical Examiner," I said, using my confident professorial voice. I could still call up that tone when necessary.

"That would be Dr. Hortense Mendoza. One moment please."

What luck! I was actually being connected to the person I wanted.

"Dr. Mendoza speaking. Can I help you?"

The woman spoke with a low musical voice that carried a slight Latino lilt.

"Yes, this is Anastasia Raven. I write for the *Cherry Hill Herald*."

"I'm familiar with your writing. I believe you've also helped bring a few people to justice unless the stories are exaggerated."

We both laughed.

"I'm not sure what you've heard," I said, "but by accident or design, I've gotten involved in more than my share of crimes."

"Why are you calling today?"

"I'm hoping you might be able to clarify the time of death in the Lyle Schoellkopf case."

"I'm not at liberty to discuss the details of an open case," Dr. Mendoza said.

I wasn't about to give up that easily. "I understand that, but I think my question is fairly general."

"You can try it and find out." She sounded a bit wary now.

"Actually, there are two parts to my question. Have you set an official time of death, and if so, is it based on medical evidence, or was it based on Charlie Dixon's statement that he heard the shot between ten-thirty and ten forty-three?"

"We have established a range of time during which that death might have occurred."

Now we were getting somewhere. "Can you give me those limits?" I pressed.

Dr. Mendoza sighed. "Can you absorb some technical information? Perhaps you could educate your crime readers as to the difficulties in establishing exact times of death."

"I'd be happy to do that." This sounded encouraging.

"Exsanguinated blood goes through five distinct stages of change: coagulation, gelation, rim desiccation, center desiccation, and final desiccation."

I typed furiously as she spoke.

"In this case, the victim died from rapid exsanguination when a bullet pierced his pulmonary vein. If you are familiar with human anatomy, you will be aware that the pulmonary vein is the only vein that carries oxygenated red blood. It's large, going directly from the lungs to the heart."

Struggling to recall biology lessons, I nodded, realized I was on the phone, and said encouragingly, "Of course. I'm with you."

"The blood exited the body quickly because of the size of the vein, but it was not pumped in spurts, because blood in a vein does not have the pressure of the heartbeat driving it."

"Are you saying there was a large pool of blood at the scene?"

"That's exactly what I'm saying, Ms. Raven. And it was not sprayed all over the room. No blood spatter patterns to analyze from arterial spray or from a weapon such as a knife or axe."

"But there's something of interest here. You began by mentioning coagulation."

"That is correct. When I arrived on the scene at eleven forty-two, there was a large pool of blood under the victim's body that was no longer spreading. It was undergoing some color changes but had not yet begun to gelatinize at the rim. That suggests that death occurred not more than ninety minutes before that time, and probably not less than thirty minutes. However, we have the police report that the body was seen at eleven-o-eight, and the victim was deceased at that time."

I was scribbling to do some fast arithmetic. "So the shooting could have happened as early as ten-twelve?"

"Look, this isn't a courtroom. I'm not going to defend these times down to an exact minute. There are environmental factors in play as well. Was the room hot, cold, humid, breezy, whatever?"

I grinned, glad that Dr. Mendoza couldn't see me. "Whatever" didn't sound quite as technical as "gelation."

She apparently wasn't sure how to interpret my silence. "Does this make sense?"

"Absolutely. And you did not rely what the pharmacist said?"

"To some extent. But eyewitness testimony is often suspect. People misremember things whether they mean to or not. And it's only my job to examine the scene as a scientist. This is without doubt a murder. Testimony that might be pertinent to someone's guilt or innocence comes into play in court, and I won't discuss that with you."

"Thank you so much for taking time to explain these things to me," I said.

"I'll look forward to reading your column. You may use this on the condition that you don't try to twist what I've said into some sort of split-second time line of the crime. I've given you generalizations based on scientific study, but they are generalizations."

"I understand perfectly," I said.

49

I was just typing "justice will best be served by keeping an open mind as regards the unfortunate death of Lyle Schoellkopf, until such time..."

The phone rang and a car pulled into the yard at the same time. I didn't recognize the number on caller ID, so I let that go to voice mail and went to the kitchen door. The driveway ends just outside that entrance.

George was slowing his gray car, the canoe still on the roof rack. The minute the car came to a stop, Jimmie jumped out of the passenger door.

"Ana, we found the stuff. You have to come with us and see it. All of it."

This made no sense, and I said as much.

"Hey! What did you do to your hair? It looks like you spilled bleach on it."

I couldn't wait for my pageboy to grow back. Change was so not cool in small towns.

The engine noise ceased, and George emerged from his side of the car.

"What's going on?" I asked. "Come in."

George and Jimmie stepped into my kitchen.

"Oh, this brings back memories," George said. "Jimmie's mother, Hazel, made such good jams. Did you know we helped save this farm?"

Jimmie gave George a sideways look. "What? My mom is Dee. Oh, you mean Grandpa Jimmie's mother. And what do you mean 'save the farm?'"

"Stories for another time, son. Right now, we need to tell Ana what we've found."

"OK," Jimmie agreed. "Well, now that Mr. Harris doesn't have to hide any more, we were driving around. He was telling me about places he knew—where his school and the canning factory were. Gosh! There's nothing left on that corner now. He said there was even a little store and a playground."

George cleared his throat.

"Right," Jimmie said. "So, since we were sharing, I decided to show him where I used to live. The trailer is still there, but no one uses it."

I thought this friendship was progressing rapidly—George and Jimmie sharing places from their childhoods. Well, Cora had been drawn immediately to this boy. Perhaps he was like his grandfather in more than looks alone.

"I was kinda shy about it, remembering the shed I built in the back, but I decided it was time to tell somebody. I'm almost grown up now, and it's just part of who I am."

Excellent maturity, but was there a point to this? "And you found something?"

"We sure did! It looks like someone is using it for some free storage space. The lean-to is filled with plastic tubs full of stuff. I don't know who owns the property now. I mean, nobody's living there, but maybe whoever bought it…"

George spoke up. "We might not have known what we were looking at, but then we saw a red kayak shoved against the back wall."

"Yup! Just like yours," Jimmie crowed.

The light dawned. "You think you've found the items that have been stolen in the last month or so."

George nodded, and Jimmie grinned from ear to ear.

"Should we call Chief Jarvi or the Sheriff's Department?" Jimmie asked. "I think most everything was stolen in town, but the Cherry Hill police don't come out here, right?"

"We'll call them both on the way there. Let's go wait in the driveway to watch things until law enforcement shows up." I grabbed my car keys and phone from the kitchen counter.

"I like your style, Ana," George said, smiling broadly.

Since the location George and Jimmie were talking about was only a mile and a half from my house, we arrived there before any official presence.

We were parked in a dry, dismal lot that surrounded the old semi-trailer which had once been converted into living space. Part of the surface had been graveled, and weeds poked through, however, they were too stunted to determine whether vehicles had been driving across the space. At the trailer, the steps had been knocked crooked from the door. One of the supports was cracked, as if a car had plowed into it. Even though the piles of junk and trash that used to be scattered across the space had been cleared away, I was filled with a sense of neglect and apathy. Whoever now owned this property wasn't living here. As several people had pointed out to me, a red Otter was an extremely common kayak. Was it possible that someone was legitimately using the shed for storage? But, why not the trailer itself if they owned the property? That would certainly be more secure. Maybe it was already full.

We waited. We'd been told not to approach the buildings until the police arrived, so we spent the time chatting. George was delighted to be staying with Cora; he couldn't get over how her love for old junk had resulted in their former high school now being filled with county treasures. I brought them up to date on the new leads in the shooting of Lyle Schoellkopf.

Ten minutes later, a Sheriff's car pulled past us and stopped near the lean-to shed that was attached to the back of the trailer. Harvey Brown stepped out of the car. I was delighted that he was the deputy who had been sent to handle this.

As I was introducing Harvey to George, a Cherry Hill squad car arrived. Kyle Appledorn had been dispatched. Village and county law enforcement often worked together, especially when cases crossed their boundary lines, as this one did.

Jimmie began explaining to Officer Appledorn why he'd been snooping around the property. He didn't have to say much, Kyle had been an officer long enough to remember Jimmie's circumstances just a few years previous.

"It wasn't even locked," I heard Jimmie say. "So, I didn't think it was hurting anything to just look inside. Because of, well... you know."

"I understand," Kyle answered. "But now you need to let us take it from here. "Tell me exactly what you saw."

Jimmie began explaining, and Harvey led George over to join them. I stayed far enough away to hopefully appear discreet but to still be able to hear what was said. George and Jimmie agreed that the only thing they could identify with certainty was the kayak. The tubs were translucent, but their contents were only shadowy shapes in the gloom of the low shed.

"Just look," Jimmie urged. "There's no cobwebs. This stuff hasn't been here very long."

"We need permission from the owner to search or a warrant," Harvey explained.

Jimmie's face fell. "Oh. Then what we found doesn't mean anything. You can't catch the thieves?"

Harvey smiled. "Hang on. The impatience of youth. We'll get someone working on finding out who owns this property and getting a warrant if we need to." He turned to me, "Ana, is there anything individual about your kayak that these gentlemen might have noticed?"

"It's pretty ordinary," I admitted. "The painter rope on the front is blue nylon if that helps,"

Harvey and Kyle looked at George and Jimmie.

Jimmie shrugged, but George nodded, squinted and said slowly, "I'm pretty sure there was a blue rope tied on that red Old Town Otter kayak."

Kyle grinned and said, "That's all we need."

"I'll get the detective working on the paperwork," Harvey said, and he walked toward his car.

50

There was nothing more we could do here. I hadn't been allowed to even look in the shed. Harvey and Kyle said they were staying right there until they had authorization to look in the buildings. We were reassured that the contents of the lean-to would be examined as soon as possible. We were also told not to tell anyone else what we'd found for fear it would tip off the thieves.

"We'll let you know, Ana," Harvey said. "We'll need you to identify the kayak. Do you think that will be possible?"

I thought a minute. "Yes, there are some scrapes that should be recognizable."

Harvey coughed. "I was thinking of something more like the serial number."

"Um. I'll check my files at home. I bought it in Jalmari at the new sports place." I didn't remember making a note of the number. To be honest, I didn't even know kayaks had serial numbers.

"It's important. Call us if you find it," Harvey instructed me.

George and Jimmie returned to Cherry Hill. Jimmie said he had an order for creampuffs that he needed to fulfill before Sunday, so he had to get busy baking. I headed home.

Once in my tiny office room I began hunting for the information that came with the kayak. If I was lucky, I'd filed it with other assorted tags and instructions that seemed important to keep, which meant in a box instead of piled somewhere. After a while, my rummaging did turn up an Old Town advertising and kayak-care folder. A half-sheet of paper printed by the sports store had been slipped inside. Along with a computer printout that listed their hours of operation, rental prices, and contact info was the phrase, "Thank you for buying your watercraft from us. We hope you never need to know your serial number, but if you do, it is...." There was an empty space and the number had been written in with marker. Hallelujah!

I wandered toward the kitchen and called the Sheriff's Department on my cell to tell them the kayak's identifier. I asked what was happening over on Alder Rd, the location that was being staked out, and was told they were trying to contact the owner. I was given no other information.

Spreading peanut butter on some bread, my mind began to ponder if the break-ins could be connected to the murder somehow. I sprinkled the peanut butter with raisins and added a second slice of bread.

Was Lyle fencing the stolen goods? It was possible that being a traveling salesman gave him a good cover for that sort of sideline. Had a meeting with the thieves gone wrong? That didn't make sense. Such a rendezvous wouldn't have taken place in Chester's apartment. Had Lyle confronted the thieves? That didn't make sense either. The places that had been burglarized were isolated storage buildings, not downtown apartments. Besides, the gun was clearly tied to the Schoellkopf family. But someone could have taken the gun away from Lyle.

The gun! The fatal shot. I wondered if Otto Osmo had timed his air compressor. Then I remembered the missed phone call and looked at the answering machine attached to the landline charger. One message. I took a bite of my sandwich and pushed the "listen" button. I heard Juli's voice say, "Hello, Ana? Sorry I missed you. Otto plugged in the compressor this morning, and it took seven minutes and twenty seconds for the tank to fill before it shut off. As I mentioned, it's really loud. Hope this helps you somehow. Call me when you want to join the Garden Club."

The machine clicked off.

I found my notebook with the times I'd been able to nail down. If the air compressor was running from 10:17 when Juli ended her call until 10:24 or 10:25, and she didn't hear anything that sounded like a gunshot after that– and I was convinced she would have heard it– then the only conclusion left was that Charlie was mistaken about the time of the first shot. Dr. Mendoza's evidence easily placed 10:20 within the ninety-minute window where the bleeding began. No one would even have to pressure her to push the envelope of possibility.

I stuffed the rest of my sandwich in my mouth and started to dial the drugstore when I realized that trying to talk to Charlie with a mouth full of peanut butter wasn't a great plan. But I was getting excited, so I chewed fast and pushed buttons. Charlie answered immediately.

I thought he might take offense at someone questioning the statement he'd given the police and also told to me. But I was mistaken.

"You know, I've been thinking about that," he said. "I'd only been looking at the spreadsheet column with the times the file was saved on the computer, but if you scroll over, there's also a column where the medication is listed, along with the name of the patient, the doctor and all kinds of data for inventory control. In fact, there's so much information that you can't see it on the screen all at one time. At least not on my screen. I don't have one of those super-wide ones."

"OK, and..."

"Well, this morning, I had to count out a prescription of Xarelto. Did you know that every single type of pill is unique?"

"Maybe," I said, noncommittally, scanning my knowledge bank in search of that bit of trivia. It didn't matter, since I knew it now.

"By noting the shape, color, pattern, and imprint on any pill or capsule, it can be identified. That said, a whole lot of them are white with some letter or number combination stamped in them."

"But a lot of them aren't?" I recalled buying some over-the-counter medication in pink capsules, and once being prescribed a yellow antibiotic.

"Right. So we don't get much call for Xarelto. There are better blood thinners, but this one is called for in cases where the patient has a-fib. I keep it in stock because Howard... um... not supposed to say, but heck, everyone knows. Anyway, City

Drug in Emily City phoned me this morning to see if I had any."

"Yes?"

"So I was thinking about it, and I remembered that I had those orange pills in my tray when I heard the shot. Odd medication, odd noise. But then I forgot. Counting pills gets rather tedious, you know."

"I suppose it does."

"I looked up the time I was filling that particular scrip, and I'm embarrassed to say it makes me look like a liar, but I assure you it was an honest mistake."

"Charlie, nobody is going to think you are dishonest. As you've said, the actual work of counting pills can be boring, and there was no way you knew that noise was significant until much later."

"Thanks for that, Ana. This means the gunshot was between 10:21 and 10:30, one prescription earlier than I thought. Do you think this is important?"

"You have no idea how important. Call Tracy right away, will you?"

Charlie promised. We hung up, and I sat in my kitchen, stunned and pleased and angry all at the same time. Chester was innocent.

51

Immediately, I dialed Adele. She would never forgive me if I didn't give her this scoop the second I was certain.

"You better sit down," I admonished.

"Oh, no. There's more bad news about my poor Chet? Can't you do something to get him out of jail? You're supposed to be helping him."

"Adele, calm yourself. We've got a new timeline, and the police will need to make it official, but it looks like Chester couldn't have done the shooting."

I heard a moaning gasp and thought Adele might have fainted.

"Are you there? Are you all right?" I was mentally kicking myself for thinking it would be acceptable to deliver such emotional information via telephone.

But Adele had gathered her wits. "Praise the Lord and pass the mixed nuts! We'll have a party to celebrate. Tell me how you figured it out."

After I explained the new information, she said, "If the murder could have been earlier, maybe Tucker isn't in the clear."

"No, remember Tracy said he was in the police station, in plain sight. I think she said he was there before ten. That's definitely too early for the shooting."

Adele sighed. "Then who?"

***

The day was heating up, and I'd spent part of the morning standing in a vacant lot leaning against a hot car. Some iced tea would be nice, but I'd have to make it. I filled the kettle and put it on the stove. While I waited for the water to boil, I dished up some ice cream and sat at the kitchen table to eat it. I didn't dare leave the room. I knew I'd forget all about the kettle if I didn't keep it in my line of sight. My brain was swirling with possibilities, or the lack of possibilities.

If neither Chester nor Tucker had killed Lyle, then who was left? Some random person who had taken the gun away from him? Pretty far-fetched. If Chester was innocent, then he had probably told the truth about the gun. He said he had bought it for his wife, Millie. But she was dead. Chester had forgotten all about it, so it was out of her possession before she died. Who might she have given it to? Lyle probably didn't want some little popgun, but maybe Eva did. Maybe Eva had stolen it from her grandmother. That seemed consistent with Eva's character.

Steam rose from the kettle's spout, and it hissed impatiently. I put the tea to steep and tried to continue my train of thought, but I couldn't come up with any answers.

I filled a tumbler with ice cubes and poured the hot tea over it, the glass changing from cold to warm and back to cold in my hand. I watched the ice melt and thought that was a good object lesson– anything that looked like a cold solid fact in this case dissolved into the murky liquid of some background I couldn't detect.

Maybe Eva shot her father. But why? Why had she come here, and what were she and Lyle doing in the apartment? Chester's apartment.

I added more ice to my glass and enjoyed a long, chilly drink.

Needing to keep my hands occupied, since my brain wouldn't cooperate, I puttered around the kitchen, washing dishes and sweeping the floor. I was contemplating washing the windows when my cell phone rang. I was saved from the unfulfilling window-washing fate. The phone screen woke up, and I was shocked to discover it was after three o'clock. The caller was deputy Harvey Brown.

"The owner of the property on Alder Road gave us permission to search the buildings," Harvey told me. "The trailer is locked, but it doesn't look as if anyone has been inside."

"Can't the owner come open it for you?" I asked.

"He lives in Indiana. He's going to overnight a key. But the important building is that lean-to, and we've emptied it. We matched your serial number to the kayak. The tubs were full of tools and auto parts. John Aho is coming by after he closes for the day to see if he can identify any of them, and we're contacting the other victims."

"You've caught the thieves?"

"Not yet. But those plastic tubs yielded some really nice prints, and so did your kayak. One of them matches the print we found on your shovel."

"This is great, Harvey!"

"It is. But I'm mainly calling to insist that you keep completely quiet about all of this. We're watching the property to see who shows up. Fingerprints are no good at all without someone to possibly match them to. These aren't in the system."

"I get it," I said. "I can keep a secret."

But I was mighty glad I hadn't told Adele, or everyone in town would know the stolen goods had been recovered.

I decided to remind George and Jimmie to keep quiet. George had given me his phone number, and I was quickly reassured that he understood the importance of keeping this information from spreading. He said he hadn't even told Cora. He did ask me if he could store his canoe beside my shed for a while so that it would be near the river whenever he wanted to paddle.

"Of course," I said. "Come over any time. I don't even need to be home. Just follow the path from the edge of the yard."

Next, I dialed Jimmie's cell, but he didn't answer, so I called his family's home phone. Beth answered.

"Jimmie's not here. After Mr. Harris dropped him off, he said he had to do some errands. He left again on his bike."

This seemed odd, since Jimmie had told us he needed to get busy baking creampuffs. However, it was quite possible he'd gone to get some missing ingredient. I called his cell again and left a voicemail. Maybe he had turned the ringer off and then forgotten.

52

Not really interested in washing windows, I spent the rest of the afternoon doodling possible plans for renovating my kitchen. The fact that George had found it familiar and comforting was nice in some ways, but mostly it confirmed my suspicion that nothing had been changed for decades except for the "new" used appliances I'd purchased.

My stomach was beginning to suggest that it was close to suppertime when my cell rang again. It was Dee, Jimmie's mother.

"Ana, is Jimmie with you?" she asked.

I almost told her we'd been at the trailer where she had lived on Alder Road, but that would probably upset her, and I would have had to explain why Jimmie and I had been there. Instead I said, "I'm pretty sure George Harris dropped him off at your house. We were all together for a while. Beth said he rode off again on his bicycle."

"Yes, Beth and Lindsey told me that, and his bike isn't here. But it's past six-thirty and I don't know where he is. He's not answering his phone. We have an arrangement– he's so stubbornly independent that I don't have a lot of choice– but he has to answer when I call. I'm afraid something is wrong."

Not wanting to alarm Dee further, I didn't tell her that he hadn't answered three hours ago either.

"Who else have you called?" I asked.

"Cora, of course. He's not there."

"All right. I'll call George too. In fact, let me give you his cell number. They seem to have hit it off."

"What do you know about George, Ana?" He's new in town. Maybe Jimmie shouldn't be spending time with him." The tension was clear in Dee's voice.

I tried to calm her. "Cora vouches for George. I just don't think he's a predator. Look, let me make some calls before you do anything else. Try not to panic, OK?"

"All right, Ana. You let me know the minute you hear anything."

Immediately, I called George. He hadn't seen Jimmie.

I thought of my theory that the boy had gone to buy some baking ingredient. I tried Adele. The store was closed by now, but I reached her at home.

Without giving me a chance to say anything– she must have recognized my number on caller ID– she squealed. "Ana! Oh, it's so wonderful. How did you know that Chet has just been released? He wants to thank you personally. Here, let me put him on the line."

This only made me impatient, but I knew this had to be the most important event in Adele's life right now. And, after all, Jimmie was a teenager. Admittedly, he was about the most wonderful teen I'd ever known, but acting erratically was a characteristic of those years. I had no doubt he'd turn up soon with good reasons and excuses for his absence. It might end up being the first time he'd ever been grounded, though. That thought made me smile.

Chester's voice came through the phone. He sounded slightly tipsy. Perhaps they'd broken out some bubbly in celebration of his release. "Ana Raven, successful sleuth! You've done it again. Let me assure you that this wonderful effort will be rewarded. I just knew that grocery store receipt would save me, and you made it so."

"I'm glad I was able to help; and I'm glad you're free again. You don't owe me anything. But I need to ask Adele an important question. Could you give me back to her?"

"Can do. Things are copasetic here. Just like old times. Hang on."

I heard whispering and perhaps the smack of a kiss. It made me cringe a little, but I reminded myself that I was not Adele's keeper.

"What's on your mind, Ana? I'm not going out tonight in case you've got some wild idea."

"Listen, Adele. No wild ideas, but Jimmie didn't come home for supper. We thought he was going to the store hours ago to buy some baking supplies. Was he there this afternoon?"

"Jimmie? Our Jimmie? I haven't seen him for days."

"Could he have slipped in and out of the store without you knowing?"

"Highly doubtful. I was the only one there after Max left at one. When would he have been there?"

"I'm not sure, but definitely after one. More like after three."

"Keep me posted. Gotta go."

Another idea had popped into my head. I called Sunny Leonard. Maybe she and Jimmie had shared chemistry stronger than I had recognized. I knew Sunny had a crush on Jimmie. Maybe some teenage spark had ignited. This made me cringe a lot harder than the thought of Chester and Adele smooching.

But Sunny was not home. For just a second my heart jumped into my throat when her grandfather said she wasn't there. But then he explained that Star had driven home from college that afternoon, and the sisters were off for an evening at the movies.

"Is there any way you could verify that?" I asked. "Sorry if this sounds rude. We can't find Jimmie Mosher, and I just need to be certain he's not out with friends."

Len said, "Let me text them. They probably have their phones off if the movie's started, but I can try. Hold on."

"Thank you," I said.

In a few seconds, Len came back on the line. "This technology stuff is just too hard for me. I think I can't do text unless I hang up. Let me call you back."

"Sure thing," I said and pressed the screen to end the call. I totally understood Len's difficulty in making phones do what he wanted, but at the same time, my insides were beginning to get queasy. If Jimmie had ridden to Hammer Bridge Town and then decided to go to the movies with the girls, surely he would have called his mother to let her know.

The phone rang in my hand.

"Hello?"

It was Len. "Ana, Sunny had forgotten to silence her phone, so she saw my message. Jimmie is not with them. She hasn't seen him since yesterday. Is anything wrong?"

"We sure hope not, Len. Thanks for helping. Do call me if you hear from him."

"I can do that, but I don't think he has my phone number."

"You're right." But then I had another thought. "Maybe he and Sunny exchanged numbers. Can you text her and tell her it's important to let us know if he contacts her?"

"Right away. Youngsters sure can be a handful."

We ended the call.

I racked my brain. Where else might Jimmie have gone?

53

"Why'd you bring that kid here? This is going to be nothing but trouble."

"I didn't– he was snooping around and saw me. I couldn't let him go then, could I?"

"Why not? He didn't know anything, but now we've got a problem."

"Look, I didn't know people were going to get hurt when we started this."

"We have to get out of town. Start collecting stuff. We'll knock him on the head and dump him and his bike in a ditch after dark. It'll look like he got hit by a car. By the time he wakes up and can talk, we'll be long gone. If he doesn't wake up, well... then so much the better."

54

The cell phone screen said it was now 7:16. I was still trying to figure out where else Jimmie could reasonably be. Maybe he had gone back to the shed on Alder Road, and the thieves had grabbed him. Nope. The police were staked out there. Both the county deputies and city police knew Jimmie well. He might have been reprimanded for interfering with their surveillance, but he would have been sent away, not detained. And if for any reason he had been held, they would have called his mother. They might have called her anyway if they'd seen him.

Maybe he sneaked into the woods behind that property to watch it for some reason of his own, and the gang had found him. This was something of a possibility although it was hard to think of a reason Jimmie would have gone back to the shed in the first place. Maybe there was still something there that belonged to him— something he didn't want to tell anyone else about, and he was trying to figure out a way to retrieve it without being detected. This made some sense. After all, I'd first met Jimmie when he was hiding money in the woods.

Maybe I should drive over there and look around. I scooped my car keys off the counter, checked my cell to be sure it was fully charged, slipped on a nylon jacket, stuffed a small flashlight in the pocket and headed for my car. I got as far as the kitchen stoop.

Right. All that would accomplish was to anger whichever law enforcement agency was watching the place. I returned to the kitchen, opened a box of crackers and began eating them for no reason other than nervousness. My appetite had disappeared.

I jumped when the phone jangled. The old-fashioned ring

tone I'd chosen sounded like some macabre movie track from the forties. Dial Ana for Alarmed. It was Dee.

"Thank goodness," she said. "Jimmie just called me. I was seriously thinking about notifying the police, although I hated to take any action before dark."

Here, at the western end of the time zone, in mid-June, there were two hours of light left. I understood that Dee had been trying hard to keep from panicking, to allow for the fact that kids lose track of time.

Dee continued, "Jimmie is so responsible. I knew there would be a good explanation."

Relief flooded through me, and my shoulders relaxed. I hadn't realized how tense I'd become.

"Where is he?" I asked.

"He's with George. His bike got a flat tire, and his phone battery had run down. George saw him walking the bike and picked him up. He's charging the phone now in the car. George is fastening the bike on the canoe rack somehow. Then he'll bring Jimmie home. They should be here before long, although I guess George was having trouble tying the bike down."

"Where are they coming from?"

"Oh!"

I groaned. "You didn't ask him where he was?"

"I was so relieved to hear his voice that I didn't think of it. He sounds fine. I'm sure he'll be home soon. But we are going to have a talk. This isn't like him, but I can't let this pass. He scared me half to death."

I told Dee to let me know when Jimmie was safely home and called George immediately.

"Where are you? Is Jimmie with you?"

55

The very first thing George did was laugh. This seemed like an odd response.

"I'm just turning on to your road with my canoe."

"Is Jimmie with you?" I repeated.

George's tone turned serious in response to the stress in mine. "No, of course not. I left him at his house this afternoon."

What was going on? My mind went blank.

"Are you there?" George asked.

"I have to hang up and call the police, now. Something is terribly wrong. Come to the house when you get here. Just walk in, and I'll tell you everything I know." I disconnected the call.

7:48. Not wanting to frighten Dee any more, I called the Sheriff's Department first. No chance I'd get Harvey now. He was probably on the stakeout. After being told I should have dialed the county-wide 9-1-1 line, I was transferred to a Detective Snelling. The good part was that I didn't have to talk to my nemesis, Detective Dennis Milford. The bad part was that I didn't know this detective at all.

The result was that they could not do anything unless a parent called it in. Not only that, but Detective Snelling was indeed new. He did not know me, Jimmie, Dee, Cora, or anyone else in Cherry Hill. His suggestion was that a fifteen-year-old was likely to be out joyriding or drinking with some friends, but admitted that since he was under sixteen the police would act on the report once his mother had made the call.

Miffed, I told him I'd have Dee file a report. But this meant I had to tell Dee what was going on.

I heard tires on gravel, and in another few seconds, George

entered the kitchen. I explained to him what we knew.

He grabbed the back of a chair and shakily lowered himself into it. "What has that boy gotten himself into?"

"Did he say anything to you that might give us a hint as to where he went?"

George's head swung slowly from side to side. "Not a single clue. He chattered about making creampuffs. Told me about his food business and some crazy idea to re-open a ruined restaurant."

If George had done something with Jimmie, he was the best actor I'd ever seen.

8:02. My guts were twisting in knots. Dee had suggested days ago that hanging out with me was potentially dangerous for her son. But that had been in relation to the singer, the singer who was now sitting in my kitchen. Either Jimmie's call had been valid, and George had done something with the boy before coming to my house, trying to appear as if nothing had happened, or... Or what? Surely, Dee knew her own son's voice. Why had Jimmie made that call? Did he lie? Why on earth would he do that?

8:05 I pushed buttons on my cell. "Dee, I think you need to sit down. I have some news that's going to be difficult to hear."

She picked up on my tone at once. Her voice quavered. "What's wrong? Is my Jimmie hurt?"

"We don't know that. But George says he hasn't seen Jimmie since early afternoon."

Dee moaned as only a mother can.

"I called the Sheriff's Department, but no one except you, his mother, can call this in. And, personally, I think you'll get a better response if you call the Cherry Hill police. The detective on duty for the county doesn't know us. I suspect they'll think he's a runaway."

"I'm telling the police to bring in George Harris for questioning! Jimmie wouldn't lie. What has George done with him?" Dee yelled at me.

My heart ached. Was it possible Dee was right? George had gone to the sink and was gulping a glass of water. He looked shaken, but not guilty.

"Look," I said, "call the police. Maybe even the State Police will get involved since Jimmie's under sixteen. But get them moving. Tell them everything, and they'll know what to do."

Dee hung up. I hadn't told her that George was sitting in my kitchen. Was I obstructing justice, interfering in an investigation? Well, I could always say I didn't realize I hadn't told her George was here. The police would have to track him down on their own. Despite how strange this all was, I couldn't see George as someone who would hurt a child.

At any rate, there wasn't anything else I could do right this minute. I was sure Dee had tried to call Jimmie's phone numerous times. There wasn't any point in my doing the same thing. I slipped my phone in a pocket.

"Come on, George," I said. "Let's get your canoe unloaded. We need to keep ourselves occupied."

8:17. The sun was dipping toward the horizon. It was already below the tops of the trees over the swamp. Only an hour of light left, I thought, admitting to myself that I was afraid there was going to be some kind of search which would be made infinitely more difficult by darkness. Silently, George released the clips on the straps that held the canoe in place. I started to get into position to help lift it down, but, of course, George was used to doing this alone. Until now, I hadn't grasped how big a man he was. He gentle demeanor had made him seem smaller. Now I realized he was over six feet tall, and strong. He lifted the canoe and swung it to the ground in one easy motion.

He grinned. "I wouldn't mind if you want to help me carry it to the cabin," he said. "Gets a little heavy on long portages."

My cell phone rang again. This time, my heart thumped, and I literally jumped, tripped over the end of the canoe, and fell flat on my back. It rang a second time.

I pulled the phone from my pocket. 8:25. I didn't recognize the number. Not Jimmie. I relaxed a little and answered. "Hello?"

"Ana, help! Jimmie's voice was distant and hollow. It sounded like he was on speaker, from whatever phone this was.

A woman yelled, "Shut that kid up!"

There were sounds of scuffling. I hit speaker on my own phone.

Another voice. This time it was a man. He sounded fairly young. He also sounded familiar. "Do it yourself. I didn't sign on to hurt anybody."

George's eyes widened as he caught the tail end of the man's statement.

Now the scuffling had escalated to crashes, followed by what I thought was the banging of an opening door being flung against a wall that had no doorstop.

Jimmie again. "Tucker's here and some lady I don't know." Splintering glass and a grunt. "No, I'm not giving it up!"

"Get that phone away from him!"

"I'm trying."

"The green cottage– north side– George knows."

A loud crash, as if the phone hit something hard. Then, deafening silence.

"Jimmie!" I yelled, pointlessly, as if I thought my voice would reach him without the aid of electronics. The call had ended, and I knew it.

George also seemed unwilling to admit the connection was gone. "I do know, Jimmie. We're coming," he bellowed. Maybe his voice could carry across the water. I'd certainly heard him singing from quite a distance. I could only hope. And pray. My renewed faith was just that, new. But anyone who wouldn't pray at a time like this had to be fiercely unwilling to even consider that divine help might be available.

As I was silently sending my plea for Jimmie into the ether, George said. "Call the police, then give me the phone. I think I can tell them how to get there by road. But we can get there faster in the canoe."

I did not want to talk to some unknown dispatcher at the 9-1-1 Center. I didn't even know where it was. Emily City, probably. The local numbers were in my contact list. I punched up the Cherry Hill Police. Even though the house where Jimmie was being held was well outside the city limits, I knew anyone who answered at the local office would take me seriously. They could call in whatever other agencies were needed.

Hallelujah! Tracy was on duty. My phone was still on speaker, and I left it that way so George could hear the conversation. I briefly explained what had happened, told her who George was, and how he fit into the picture. Then I handed the phone to George.

I listened to him giving her directions to a green cottage with brown shutters on the north side of the river and realized two things. First, it was a long, complicated drive from Cherry Hill, following a maze of dirt two tracks. Secondly, George had a pretty good idea of the roads needed to get there, but he certainly wasn't positive about some of the many forks and turns where the primary dirt road split into myriad dusty lanes, old logging roads, and ATV tracks as it approached the river.

Tracy asked him if he knew the address or who the owner was.

"No, ma'am. I'm sorry. I'm pretty sure there's one of those green fire number posts in the driveway, but I don't know what it is. I saw all these summer houses mostly from the river, and I wouldn't remember the number anyway. But I did drive to that one once. I was looking for a boat launch site where I could put in my canoe."

"Is there a public access at the end of that road?"

"There is not. No, I turned around and drove back to explore another fork in the road."

"That's some help. We can eliminate the official access roads. All right, Mr. Harris. Thank you. Please stay on the line."

We heard an electronic sound, as if we'd been put on hold. I knew this meant Tracy was setting things in motion.

In a minute or so, she said, "Can Ana hear me too?"

"She's right here. We've got you on speaker."

Tracy said she had come to the office when the initial call from Dee had been forwarded to her cell phone. They had already called the State Police, and she'd talked to Detective Snelling, explaining to him that Jimmie was not some average, troubled teenager. All three agencies were actively looking for the teen, and she had now given them all this current information.

I explained that Dee was not up to date on what we had just learned about her son's whereabouts, and Tracy said their office would notify Jimmie's mother. She said the State Police had contacted a resource person to help guide and comfort Dee as the situation unfolded.

"This person is with Dee now?" I asked, knowing how frantic she would be.

"She's en route to Dee's house from Emily City. That's the closest one."

While Tracy had been filling me in, George had poked me in the arm and gestured that he was taking the canoe to the river. He pointed to me and then himself and pantomimed paddling. He grabbed his paddle from the car and took off at a trot, dragging the canoe along the path.

When I ended the call with Tracy it was 8:47. Only thirty minutes until dark.

I ran down the path to catch up with George. He was just getting ready to launch the canoe.

"Do you have a paddle?" he asked. "With two of us to fight the current, we can get there lots faster than anyone can drive there. It's really close from here."

Momentarily, my heart sank. The cabin was locked. I'd fixed the broken door after my kayak was taken. Would it be faster to break in or to run back to the house for the keys? Then I remembered I was still wearing the jacket I'd put on when I thought of going to look for Jimmie on Alder road. I reached in the pocket and displayed the keys triumphantly.

In another minute, we were on the water. George was expertly steering from the stern, and I was awkwardly manning the bow position with my kayak paddle. It was the only paddle I owned. Jimmie had left his Louisville Slugger in the cabin, and it now rested in the bottom of the canoe.

57

We pushed off into the gathering dusk. Trees grew close along the river and the last rays of sunlight struggled to penetrate the gloom. Water lapped at the bow of the canoe. Something of significant size splashed into the water behind us, perhaps a muskrat. The air was cooler here; I was glad for the jacket. The fusty scent of drying algae tickled my nose, but informed me that the river level had gone down, leaving muddy banks and damp tangles of trapped branches. This was good news. The high, fast-moving springtime river had given way to the lazier and safer flow of summertime. We needed all the help we could get. We reached the center of the current, and George turned the canoe into it.

"We have to go upstream," he said. "Paddle at your own pace, and I'll keep us on course."

I could feel the power in George's arms as we moved steadily against the moving water. "What's our plan? Do we have one?" I asked.

"Very soon, we're going to need to keep quiet. Sound carries on the water, and that house isn't far. We'll have to communicate mostly with signals, but it's hard to plan until we know what we're up against."

"At least two people," I said.

"Right, and they are either now on high alert or in a state of confusion. Hard to tell. Sounds like that young man is pretty resourceful."

I chuckled. "That he is. But maybe they've restrained him by now." I hated the thought of what else they might have done.

"Or maybe he got away. There's no way to tell until we get there."

"I think our primary goal should be to rescue Jimmie, and leave his captors to the authorities."

"I agree," George said, steering the canoe to the left at a fork. This wasn't the main channel of the river. The water was calmer and we made better time. "Now we need to keep our voices down."

We followed several more twists of the river, alternately paddling in swifter and calmer water. I'd explored the river a bit in my kayak, but never at night. Some of the backwaters changed from year to year. I had to rely completely on George's sense of location.

An owl hooted. We were back in the main channel and a light winked through the trees on the north bank.

Suddenly George executed a sweep and the canoe turned left, toward the light. The bow of the canoe bumped a dock and I automatically reached out to pull us alongside. I stowed my unwieldy paddle and scrambled to the rough planks while George held us steady. The sun had not completely set, but the woods were full of deep shadows. I could now see that the light we'd seen was shining through a window, but it wasn't the bright glow I would have expected from a lamp. I wrapped the painter line attached to the bow around a bollard on the dock.

"Down," George hissed.

I complied quickly then turned my head just enough to look toward the house. A door in the cottage had opened, and Tucker was carrying a suitcase toward a car with its trunk open. The light was fading every second. I could barcly make out colors but the car certainly looked orange to me. Eva! The engine was running. This was good news for us; the sound would cover our approach.

Tucker returned to the house, and I sprinted to reach a window, around the corner from the door. I was almost there when I tripped on a root and went sprawling. Pain coursed through my right ankle, and I clapped a hand over my mouth to keep from crying out. Nausea and weakness spread through my entire body. I rolled dand grasped the ankle, clamping my lips tightly shut. I would not even moan. I would not.

I saw George approaching, crouched and holding the bat in

both hands, ready for action. Now, he came to me and knelt down.

"I'm fine," I whispered. "Just give me a minute to catch my breath." I hoped it was true.

Tucker appeared again, heading for the car with a box. He apparently had no idea anyone else was around. He proceeded without caution and dropped the carton in the trunk. While his back was toward us, George had slunk around the corner and was now in position behind a bush. Tucker straightened.

I didn't even see George move. He was as stealthy as the approaching darkness. He wrapped one arm around Tucker's neck and placed the other hand over his mouth. Silently, Tucker slid to the ground. The ease with which George had accomplished this move made me suspect he had been in the military.

I'd managed to crawl to the window and was looking into the living room of a cozy cottage. George returned to my side.

"He'll be out for a while, but the woman will come looking for him," George whispered.

I pointed at the window. The yellowish light inside came from a camping lantern with failing batteries. It barely illuminated the room. Maybe the owner of the cottage had the electricity turned off when they weren't there.

Jimmie was facing us, tied to a straight chair that had been placed so he was distanced from any other piece of furniture. My guess was this was the result of whatever roguery he'd managed earlier to snag a phone and call me. A twisted red bandana was tied around his mouth.

A young woman, probably Eva since I knew the car was hers, was crouched with her back toward us. She was burning papers in a fireplace.

A window on the adjacent wall was broken, and a bookcase had been tipped over. Books splayed across the floor. A overturned bowl sat cockeyed on the pine flooring, a brown gelled mess oozing from beneath it, and the spoon had been flung several feet away. It looked as if no attempt had been made to straighten up after what had to be the struggle we'd heard on the phone.

I waved my arm, and Jimmie saw the motion. His eyes opened wide, but he was quick to replace his surprise with the watchful, patient look he'd worn a moment before. He jerked his head in the direction of the door.

58

I gave Jimmie a thumbs-up, not sure if he could see the smaller gesture as the darkness was deepening.

George handed me the bat and sidled around the corner, toward the door. I limped along behind him, gritting my teeth and mentally chastising myself for the fall which had rendered me nearly useless. Tucker still lay unconscious on the ground.

We reached the door, and George extended his right arm and pushed me back against the exterior wall. He pointed two fingers toward his eyes and then one finger toward the body slumped behind the car. I got it. He wanted me to watch Tucker while he went after Eva. I nodded.

We waited. The sound of the running engine covered most of the night noises. The owl hooted again, but I couldn't hear the gurgling water, crickets, or more importantly, anything from inside the cottage.

George laid a calming hand on my shoulder. Tucker didn't stir from where he had fallen.

We waited for what seemed far too long, but it probably wasn't more than a few minutes. I heard the doorknob turn and saw a sliver of orange light flash across the grass. The sliver widened to a strip broken by the shadow of a woman.

"What are you doing?" Eva called into the night. She opened the door farther and the light caught Tucker's still frame. "What the...?"

Eva stepped onto the concrete stoop.

George's hand shot out and snagged Eva's neck. She screamed, but then she too, crumpled into a heap.

I dropped the bat and limped as fast as I could across the room to release Jimmie. He hugged me. "I knew you'd come.

Maybe I should have called my mom, but she wouldn't know how to get here fast. They made me call her before–I hoped she'd figure out it wasn't true."

"You need to thank George for everything," I said as he entered the room.

Jimmie started jabbering, either from nervousness or just a desire to tell us everything he'd heard.

"They told me all about it. Eva decided to make sure she got her grandfather's money, you know, that guy I met at the church social. But she knew he wouldn't give it to her. She met Tucker at a party, and he looked just like her grandad. So they cooked up this scheme to get him to leave all his money to this new-found grandson, and then they would split it. She gave him stuff from when she was little to use to prove that he was Lyle's son. Even a picture that didn't show her face."

"Hold on, Jimmie," I said. "You can tell me more later. The police are on the way, but they don't have good directions. It might take them a while to find us. We need to call them and tie up Tucker and Eva..."

A shadow loomed behind George. Tucker stood there with the baseball bat raised over his head. I lunged at him in an attempt at a tackle, but pain shot up my entire leg, and I didn't hit him hard.

It deflected his aim just enough. Instead of a solid hit that would have fractured George's skull, the bat caught him on the left shoulder and he staggered forward with a groan. But then he reached across and took hold of the end of the bat with his right hand, pulling Tucker off balance.

"Go," George yelled. "Take Jimmie in the car and find the police. Bring them here. I've got this guy."

"I know the road, Ana. Let's go."

Jimmie practically dragged me across the room, my ankle on fire. We stopped for only a few seconds to hastily tie Eva's hands and feet with the bandana and ropes that Jimmie had gathered up while Tucker, George and I were tussling. At least Tucker wouldn't get much help from her for a few minutes. I hoped that would give us all enough time. I'd seen George in action and didn't doubt he could handle Tucker without our aid.

Jimmie raced to the car, and I hobbled as fast as I could. I slid into the driver's seat, shifted into gear, and put pressure on the accelerator pedal. Unbearable pain shot up my leg.

When I woke up, I was sprawled awkwardly in the passenger seat and Jimmie was driving. He grinned at me. "I guess I'm a criminal now. Driving at night with an unapproved adult."

"Just keep going," I said through clenched teeth. "Find whoever is on the way to help."

"Call Chief Jarvi," Jimmie suggested. "She can tell us where the car is that's looking for us. They took my phone away and busted it."

Great idea! Apparently my brain wasn't working too well.

I made the call, and Tracy was able to contact the State Police car that was searching the back roads on the north side of the river where we were. With the help of the GPS locator on my phone, within ten minutes, we were all headed back toward the green cottage, with Jimmie proudly leading the way. Tracy relayed the information that George was there alone, trying to subdue Tucker when we had left him. We were told to stay in the car once we got to the house.

"We can do that," I agreed.

"I explored all these roads on my bike. I know how to get everywhere over here now," Jimmie boasted.

Well, maybe it wasn't boasting. Maybe it was just true.

Since stealth was no longer an issue, when Jimmie turned in the driveway, the police hit their siren and flashers. The cruiser pulled past us, and two officers jumped out and approached the house, guns drawn. They positioned themselves on each side of the door, which was still open. But Eva was no longer on the stoop.

59

In a moment, one of the officers stepped outside and waved us in. I couldn't imagine what had happened.

When we entered the living room, George was sitting on the pine board floor in the middle of the room, holding his head in his right hand. A visible lump had risen on the left side, above the temple. Neither Tucker nor Eva was there.

"EMTs are en route," the officer squatting beside George said. "Just stay down, now, sir. If you feel up to it, can you tell us what happened?"

"I'm sure my head is hard enough to withstand another bump."

"Nevertheless, you just hold still." The officer put a hand on George's shoulder.

George rubbed his right hand over the giant goose egg, but I noticed that he was strongly favoring his left side, the one Tucker's first blow had connected with. He held his left arm stiffly in front of his chest.

"What about your shoulder?" I asked, sitting down on George's other side, both to comfort him and to take the weight off my ankle. I tried not to let my pain show.

"I think I might have a broken collarbone," he admitted. "Nothing serious."

"Sir, what happened?" the officer urged.

"Sure, sorry. Well, I was getting the best of the young man, even with only one arm. He doesn't know anything about hand-to-hand combat. But then that woman crawled in the house on all fours. I guess she picked up the bat, even with her hands tied, and smacked me one. That's the last I remember."

"So the two suspects fled?"

"As far as I know," George said.

"Did they have a vehicle?"

Jimmie spoke up. "They did, but that's what we're driving. So they must be on foot now."

George looked up. "Check the dock. See if my canoe is gone."

Jimmie ran outside.

The officer continued, "So you two came across the river to rescue this young man?"

"That's the truth. I knew we'd be able to get here faster than anyone in a car," George said.

"It's gone!" Jimmie burst into the room. "They're on the river."

"Or they turned the canoe loose to make us think that, and they are on foot," I said.

The standing officer spoke into his shoulder mic. "Suspects are either on the river in a canoe, or fleeing the scene on foot. Not observed on access road."

Jimmie couldn't contain himself. "I bet they went downstream. It would be the fastest way to leave. There's a takeout at the end of the two-track that's behind Stumpy Grimes' old farm. Then the next place to beach a canoe would be on the east side of Cherry Hill, on Meadow Street. And if you don't get out there, then you have to at the park, right in town, because you can't go through the mill race. It's dark. They wouldn't know about Stumpy's. But they could steal a car in town."

"Good thinking, son," the officer said. "Do you have any estimate of how long it might take them to get there?"

"I can answer that," George said. "We're only about two or three miles from town as the crow flies, but it's more like five on the river. If they know how to paddle, they could make it in a couple of hours. If they don't know what they're doing, it'll be at least three, if they make it at all. They might get caught on something and capsize."

I recalled Charlie's lecture on strainers and heard the wail of a siren in the distance. With a GPS location to home in on, the ambulance was having no trouble finding us. In a few minutes, medical help arrived, followed by Sheriff's officers who would secure the scene. George insisted his head would be fine, but the broken collarbone was confirmed, and he was carried away. He said he'd call Cora and keep her up to date. We promised to visit if they kept him in the hospital.

"Let's get you home, young man," the officer in charge said. "We'll need a complete statement from you, but it can wait until tomorrow. I think your mother is pretty anxious to see you right now."

"What about my bike?"

"You can get it tomorrow, son."

He turned to me. "Ditto for your statement. We'll contact you in the morning. How did you get here?"

"In the canoe with George. I'll need a ride home."

He nodded, and we headed for the police car. I tried to keep from limping. I'd managed to keep the EMTs from learning about my twisted ankle, and I planned to keep it that way.

Jimmie gave the officer his address, and he couldn't stop talking as we traveled toward his house.

"I heard all about it, Ana. Tucker and Eva were having a big fight because everything was going wrong, and when I showed up, *bam*, everything got even more complicated. Do you think I'll get to testify in court?"

I contemplated that, but he didn't wait for an answer.

"Eva just wanted Tucker to convince Mr. Schoellkopf, the old guy, to change his will. When Tucker inherited the money, they were going to split it. She wasn't even afraid that Tucker might kill her to be able to keep it all, and maybe she was right because he kept yelling at her that he wasn't going to be held responsible for hurting anyone."

"He sure seemed OK with trying to hurt George," I pointed out.

"Well, maybe... But he didn't want to kill anyone," Jimmie insisted.

"But what about Lyle, the man who was shot? Tucker told us he was dead already."

Jimmie laughed. "I think that Eva was crazy. She paid somebody to show Tucker a fake death certificate so that he'd believe it, and be more likely to help her with her plan."

"But how long were they going to wait?" I wondered aloud. "What if Chester found out that Lyle was alive."

"Exactly! I think Eva was planning to kill her grandfather after the will was changed. She's really bad news. But then Lyle showed up and their layout got totally messed up. They had to get him out of the way, and they tried to make it look like Mr. Schoellkopf was the one who did him in."

"What were you doing at the cabin," I asked.

"After George dropped me off, I had a flash. I remembered seeing an orange car there, and you'd told us that it might be important. So I went to check it out."

"Jimmie Mosher! You need to use your head before you go off doing dangerous things alone."

He ducked his head. "Yeah, I guess I should have told somebody." Then he lifted his chin and grinned. "But it all turned out fine."

The confidence of youth. There were a lot of pieces of this story that still didn't make sense to me, but we were pulling into Jimmie's driveway. I'd have to wait for answers.

<h1 style="text-align:center">60</h1>

Before we had come to a complete stop, Dee was running down the driveway.

Jimmie hopped out of the car and hugged his mother.

"What have you done? What have you done?" Dee keened, over and over.

But Jimmie was grinning about as widely as possible. "Aw, Mom," he said, pulling away and holding her by the shoulders. "It wasn't so bad, and we caught the people who were trying to cheat Mr. Schoellkopf. They were the ones who killed his son."

"Don't you try to convince me you weren't in danger, James Jedediah Mosher. Now get in that house." She actually smacked him on the behind.

Jedediah, huh? His great-grandfather's name. Jimmie flashed me a triumphant look, but Dee's gaze was darker. "I'll talk to you later, Ana," she said. I was glad she didn't mention my hair.

The State Troopers continued toward my house, south of town. We didn't speak much. As we passed Alder Road, I pointed. "Turn left at the next drive."

"The officer in the passenger seat swiveled toward me. "That's quite some young man. Your police chief told us a few of his exploits."

"He's pretty special to us," I agreed. "I live in the house his great-great-grandfather built."

"Now, that's something."

I was just getting out of the car when the radio squawked. "Suspects apprehended at Meadow Street. Currently being transported to Forest County jail."

"Roger that," the officer responded.

So, just like that, the adventure was over. Thankfully, my status as crime reporter meant that I'd learn the missing pieces of the puzzle, but not tonight. The adrenalin was wearing off, and I'll admit I was beat. When I realized I'd have to rewrite my column for the next edition of the paper, I was even more whipped. But first, ice on my ankle and sleep.

***

Detective Snelling called me in the morning and told me to come give my statement as soon as possible. He said all paperwork was being coordinated through his office.

My ankle throbbed, but it didn't seem as if anything was broken. I iced it and then wrapped it with an ace bandage.

Around eleven, as I was leaving the Sheriff's Office, Dee and Jimmie were entering. Again, he grinned at me, but his mother glared and pushed past me without saying a word. I was pretty sure I'd be held responsible for Jimmie's decisions for a while.

My next stop was the grocery store. I wondered if Adele would be working, or if she had left the business in the care of someone else for a day of celebrating with Chester. I didn't have to wonder long. They were in the office together, sipping wine and nibbling cheese and fruit from the deli.

"Come join us!" Chester beckoned.

"Yes, do," Adele echoed. "Tracy called to give us the official word that the real murderer has been caught, and Chet is totally in the clear. No grocery receipt needed."

"We're drinking to my freedom, but we don't want to get too wiggy, since the most guilty party seems to be my granddaughter."

"It really wouldn't look right," Adele added primly. She pulled another plastic wine glass from an opened package and began to fill it.

I waved her off at about half way. "I haven't even had lunch," I protested.

"Neither have we. Let's fix that," Chester said. He left the office and headed into the store. I elevated my throbbing ankle and rested it on his vacant chair.

Adele leaned in close to me and said. "Chet's been through the wringer in the last couple of weeks, and he means so much to me, but..."

"But what, Adele?"

"We were talking last night until very late. He wants me to leave the store and go back to California with him. I just..." Her eyes flicked to the large convex mirror that allowed her to see down the aisles. "Customer, be right back." She headed for the cash register.

I popped a cube of cheese in my mouth and contemplated Cherry Hill without Adele. I hoped she was leading up to a decision to stay here, in the community that appreciated her talents and tolerated her nosiness. I feared that in California she'd be just one more stout aging female, only then she'd have money. And didn't California have a code that required women to stay slim and tanned? Well, Cora had told me Adele already had money. Enough to stave off West Coast temptations?

Chester returned with more items– sandwiches cut in triangles, crackers, a veggie pack, and fancy chocolates wrapped in gold foil.

"We're in luck. Adele makes up extra deli trays for the weekends. People like 'em for parties, and we're partying." He popped the lids on the plastic containers.

I swung my foot back to the floor.

Adele returned to the office, and we resumed chatting and celebrating. I brought them up to date on everything Jimmie had told me.

"But what about the DNA test?" Chester asked. "I just don't understand that."

"I know," I agreed. "And how did this all go down in your apartment?"

We were trying to figure it out when the front door banged against the wall. This required a lot of force, since it was tethered with a long spring. The bell clanged harshly, its music ruined as the bow and clapper were smashed against the wood. Jimmie ran into the office. He face was twisted with teenage anguish. Dee was on his heels. She looked less devastated, but definitely stressed.

"Ana! It's so horrible." His voice cracked and jumped an octave on the word "horrible."

61

"What on earth?" Adele said.

I stood and put a hand on Jimmie's shoulder.

His mom wrapped him in a hug from behind. "It's quite a blow," Dee said.

"Jimmie, tell us what's going on. Are the police charging you with something? Are you in trouble for driving the car? I'll explain that I passed out. Surely they can't fault you for getting away from a violent situation."

"No, that's all OK. It's worse, Ana. After we were done at the Sheriff's Department, the realtor called my mom. The Cherry Blossom has been sold!"

My head shifted into slow motion. This didn't compute. "You're telling me that someone has bought the restaurant property? I thought your family had first option."

Dee said. "It wasn't anything formal. We just never thought anyone else would have an interest. There's plenty of other vacant commercial land nearby. Why would someone want that particular piece? One where they would probably need to bulldoze a building."

I looked at Adele and Chester. Adele's face registered the same shock and sadness I was feeling. Chester was trying to keep the corners of his mouth from twitching upwards.

I lost my temper. "You! You come here from California and disrupt Adele's life. It seems you didn't commit any crime, but somehow fraud and murder tracked you down and caused Jimmie all kinds of trouble when he tried to help solve things and keep your golden butt out of jail. And now, you have the audacity to smile at his misfortune? Maybe you haven't taken his dream to re-open his father's restaurant seriously. Well, let me tell you..."

Now Chester was actually laughing. He reached out a hand like an officer stopping traffic. "You don't understand." He stopped laughing, straightened his face and coughed.

Adele's mouth was puckered in displeasure. She cared as much about Jimmie as I did, and it couldn't be making her happy to see someone she liked make fun of him.

Chester stuffed a hand into his pocket. He turned to Adele. "Last night, after I got the call that put me completely in the clear, what did I do?"

Her eyebrows scrunched together. "You went out. Said you had something to do. You were very mysterious."

"Indeed. First I made a phone call and got someone out of bed. Then I met with that person and obtained these in exchange for a little pocket change from my golden butt." He removed his hand from the pocket, and from his fingers dangled a set of keys. He presented them to Jimmie.

"I don't understand," Jimmie said.

"The Cherry Blossom is yours. Put that energy to work."

This called for chocolate. I grabbed one and held the package out to the others.

***

The following Tuesday morning, when the police reports were complete, and I'd received my copies, I sat at my desk writing my crime column at the last possible minute before the deadline. The article for the paper had to be sanitized with all kinds of disclaimers about alleged charges, and suspected motives and activities, because the trials of Eva Schoellkopf and Tucker Metcalf had not yet taken place. But off the record, I can tell you what actually happened.

Actually, Tucker probably wasn't going to have a trial. He flipped on Eva and made a full confession. He didn't want anything to do with being involved in a murder, although he was still facing serious charges, and unless his lawyer was exceptionally adept at plea bargaining, he might go down for the murder anyway, as part of the felony fraud.

As Jimmie had told me, Eva had run into him one day, and was struck by his uncanny resemblance to her grandfather. She cooked up the scheme to get Chester to leave his money to this long-lost grandson. She promised to split the money with Tucker for helping her. Given the rest of Eva's evil plans, I had to wonder if she was contriving to keep it all.

They had followed Chester to Cherry Hill and decided a small town full of hicks was a perfect place to make their story look plausible.

Eva supplied Tucker with pictures and items from her childhood. She paid a friend to fake a death certificate for Lyle and show it to Tucker to help convince him their scheme would work, that Lyle didn't stand in the way of the inheritance. Tucker thought maybe she was planning to kill her father all the time, but Eva had clammed up and refused to say anything.

However, Tucker was proud of his own addition to the scam. He had Eva take a DNA test, then he downloaded a copy of the results and just photoshopped the document to make it look like his own. If no one checked for the original results, it looked 100% genuine.

Eva broke in to a cottage that hadn't yet been opened for the summer to use as a base of operations. But she had Tucker get a room at the Sleep Lodge as part of his cover to interact with his supposed grandfather.

Then things began to go wrong for them. Lyle appeared in Emily City on a sales trip for Triton Pacific.

Lyle had also booked a room at the Sleep Lodge. Tucker recognized Lyle from pictures Eva had showed him, but Lyle did not see Tucker. That resulted in the first big fight between the two con artists, since it proved Eva had lied to Tucker at least once, about the death certificate.

Lyle's presence was a real problem. Without telling Tucker her plans, Eva decided to kill her father sooner rather than later and make it look like Chester had done it. She had the derringer that her grandfather had originally purchased which made it easy to frame him.

She convinced Tucker to get hold of Chester's keys and make a copy of the one for his apartment. Tucker said he managed that on the afternoon they went shopping together.

Then Eva went to meet her father. She claimed she had a desire to apologize for her behavior and make amends. She invited him to "her" apartment, which of course was really Chester's.

When they got to the apartment, Chester was not there. So Eva didn't have to invent anything complex on the spot. She simply turned the gun on Lyle and shot him. She was leaving when she heard the door at the bottom of the stairs opening. She left the gun on a step and quickly slipped out by way of the fire escape, walking boldly to her car on Meadow Street. Juli had apparently been digging, and hadn't seen her in the alley.

Taking Lyle's keys and leaving them in his car was just a fanciful touch to confuse the police.

No question about that. Eva and Tucker succeeded in confusing everyone. Jimmie was the no-questions-asked hero for remembering that Blast Orange Acura, even if he should have let the police follow up on it rather than trying to solve the mystery alone.

And then there was George. Cherry Hill's own George Harris. Despite being temporarily overcome, he had saved all of us with his combat knowledge.

62

In light of the arrests of Eva and Tucker, the capture of the local thieves slipped into the shadows. To the surprise of no one, it turned out to be teenagers trying to earn some easy cash by grabbing portable and marketable goods. Three boys and a girl from Shagway were apprehended. They had managed to sell only a few of the items they'd stolen; almost everything was returned to the rightful owners within a week. My kayak was once again locked in the cabin on the banks of the Petite Sauble River, within the floodplain known as Dead Mule Swamp.

***

A month later, Dee was speaking to me again. She knew what had happened wasn't really my fault, but Jimmie's mulish independence was going to continue to make her life interesting.

I kept my promise to have a campfire that everyone could enjoy. Jimmie and his family arrived early, building up a fire, and hauling a cooler of drinks and packages of marshmallows, graham crackers and chocolate bars from my house.

George came next, not alone, and not by water. He still wore a sling. Collarbones don't heal quickly for seniors, even ones in as good condition as George. Sunny Leonard carried the case which held his mountain dulcimer, and Paddy the Irish Setter pranced at her side. Jimmie and the girls ran to greet her and fuss over the friendly dog.

After receiving many hugs, Paddy ran to me and nuzzled my hand. He hadn't forgotten me.

Cora and Jerry strolled down the path right behind George. When they reached the clearing, Jerry unfolded the two nylon chairs he'd been carrying and placed them opposite my two rough benches.

Adele appeared last, alone. She was huffing a bit from the walk, and she also carried a folding chair.

I made a mental note to buy a few to stash in the cabin.

The kids couldn't wait for the fire to burn down to coals. They quickly loaded up the toasting forks, which I did own, and extended stacks of white sugary blobs into or near the flames.

Sunny helped George extract the dulcimer from the case, and he slipped out of the sling and began strumming softly, moving his left arm as little as possible. The water lapped at the banks of the river, and a great blue heron rose in a whoosh of wingbeats from a sandbar on the opposite shore. Paddy gave a doggy yawn and flopped on his side– a large hairy red puddle with legs.

Lindsey giggled and ran from the fire, waving a flaming marshmallow in a desperate effort to extinguish it. Sunny chased her. "Careful you don't set your hair on fire. Just blow on it." She captured the younger girl and they puffed until the charred remains sagged down the fork.

"It's OK. I like them burned," Lindsey said.

"Have you heard from Chester?" I asked Adele.

"Yes, he called me yesterday," my friend said. "He's home and settling in to manage his newest business venture. He's taking subscriptions to a Fruit-of-the-Month Club, and sending packages to those who sign up at exorbitant prices. He'll be richer than ever in another year."

I sighed. "Any regrets that you stayed here?"

"None at all," Adele said. "I love my store. I love that all of you love Cherry Hill. You are my family. Chet is special, but not marry-me special."

"We'd hate to lose you," Cora said, and Jerry echoed the thought.

The prospect that Chester was going to be richer than ever was intriguing. Apparently, he had a Midas touch. His fortune had grown even though his inheritance gave him a leg up. Not only had he bought the Cherry Blossom Restaurant for Jimmie, putting it in trust with his mother's name until he turned eighteen, but he'd rewarded both George and me, generously. I didn't need the money, but George had decided to stay in the area. He was going to repair his old home, and that would take a lot of financing. George refused to accept my share of the reward outright, but I was planning devious ways to make sure it was funneled to him. I'd already opened an account in his name at the lumber yard, and anonymously deposited a nice non-refundable sum.

Cora nibbled on a graham cracker, while I chose a chocolate bar. This is why Cora weighs barely a hundred pounds, but if I wasn't careful, I might end up looking more like Adele.

George began singing the first song I'd heard on the river, "Deep river, my home is over Jordan..." However, he no longer sounded sad. We all joined in, and the kids quickly picked up the words and tune. Paddy's ears twitched, then relaxed.

"Can you do 'The Cherry Blossom Rag?'" Beth asked. "It's our school song."

Laughing, George answered. "I remember! But I haven't tried it on a dulcimer. You'll have to give me time to practice." Nevertheless he managed to pluck out the opening notes.

Adele leaned forward. "I can't hold this news any longer. Chet shared the final irony with me yesterday."

The sticky-fingered kids crowded around her. The rest of us leaned forward. I couldn't imagine what else there was to tell. Tucker had pled guilty to reduced charges: conspiracy to commit fraud, and assault for breaking George's collarbone, but all the rest of the blame had fallen on Eva. She was still awaiting trial, but there wasn't much question about the eventual outcome. Eva wasn't going to be much of a factor in Chester's future. Not that she had been for quite some time.

"Spill it!" I demanded.

"Just on a whim, I guess, Tucker had his own DNA tested. He got the results back two days ago and contacted Chet."

With this opening, I began to anticipate what was coming, but it was still a jaw-dropper.

"Tucker really is Chet's grandson." Adele paused for effect.

Cora snapped to attention. "What?"

Paddy raised his head and woofed.

"It's true," Adele said. "Lyle actually was sowing wild oats on his business trips."

Now it was my turn to share another piece of information I had learned. Tracy kept Lyle's burner phone, and a couple of weeks later there had been an incoming call. It was from a private detective who had been hired by Lyle to track down a lost son. Lyle was not as ignorant of his extra offspring as he had led people to believe. He had followed the detective's trail to Tucker, but had not yet made any contact.

"What's Chester doing with that information?" Jerry asked.

"Well, I'm told Tucker probably can't inherit anyway, since he committed fraud against his grandfather. And he's just lucky he isn't being charged with accessory to murder. If they charge him with that in the future, he's definitely out. Chet is re-writing his will to be sure that all his money goes to the California Fruit Growers Charity Fund. He's specifically leaving only a thousand dollars to Tucker, in case the charges are dropped somehow, and also one thousand each for any other legitimate claims presented as being his heir. It's a possibility, given Lyle's habits."

George strummed a harsh and dramatic chord. "Karma has sharp teeth."

The fire was dying down and dusk was settling on my little patch of heaven.

Beth and Lindsey reached for the marshmallow bag.

Jimmie and Sunny stood and wandered in the direction of the river. Paddy shook himself and bounded after them.

Cora leaned over and rested a hand on George's good shoulder– two childhood friends, once again reunited.

I smiled at Jerry and Dee as the sun slipped between the trees to the west.

This moment was filled with great contentment, but I felt as if I needed a vacation. There had been too many murders in Dead Mule Swamp.

The eighth Anastasia Raven story will be *Vacation from Dead Mule Swamp*

PUBLISHED WORKS BY JOAN H. YOUNG

Non-Fiction:
> North Country Cache: Adventures on a National Scenic Trail (2005 Independent Publishers, third place Regional Non-fiction)
> North Country Quest: Completing my National Scenic Trail Adventure
> Would You Dare?
> Devotions for Hikers
> Get Off the Couch with Joan
> Fall Off the Couch Laughing
> Would You Dare?

Fiction:
Anastasia Raven Mysteries
> News from Dead Mule Swamp
> The Hollow Tree at Dead Mule Swamp
> Paddy Plays in Dead Mule Swamp
> Bury the Hatchet in Dead Mule Swamp
> Dead Mule Swamp Druggist
> Dead Mule Swamp Mistletoe
> Dead Mule Swamp Singer

Dubois Files Mysteries for Children
> The Secret Cellar
> The Hitchhiker
> The ABZ Affair
> The Bigg Boss
> The Lonely Donkey

Other
> Accidentally Yours- a chaotic collection of short works

ABOUT THE AUTHOR

Joan H. Young has enjoyed the out-of-doors her entire life. Highlights of her outdoor adventures include Girl Scouting, which provided yearly training in camp skills, the opportunity to engage in a ten-day canoe trip, and numerous short backpacking excursions. She was selected to attend the 1965 Senior Scout Roundup in Coeur d'Alene, Idaho, an international event to which 10,000 girls were invited. She rode a bicycle from the Pacific to the Atlantic Ocean in 1986, and on August 3, 2010 became the first woman to complete the North Country National Scenic Trail on foot. Her mileage totaled 4395 miles. She often writes and gives media programs about her outdoor experiences.

In 2010 she began writing more fiction, including several award-winning short stories. *Dead Mule Swamp Singer* is the seventh story in the Anastasia Raven mystery series.

Visit booksleavingfootprints.com for more information.